"Tabbie's original and unusual plots and storylines make for a really intriguing read."
                      Dave Andrews, Presenter, *BBC Radio Leicester*

"The master of supernatural suspense."
                      Peter J Bennett, *Author*

"The books are catching, they keep you thinking, and make you 'look outside the box'. I enjoy reading Tabbie's books in my limited down time."
                      Anne Royle and Spook (my four legged glasses).
                    Founder *Pathfinder Guide Dog Programme*

Sever His Member

Other Books by this Author

THE JENNY TRILOGY
White Noise is Heavenly Blue
The Spiral
Choler

A Fair Collection
The Unforgiveable Error
No-Don't!
Above The Call
A Bit Of Fresh
A Bit Of Spare
The Paws Of Spiritual Justice

Visit the author's website at:
www.tabbiebrowneauthor.com

Sever His Member

Tabbie Browne

Copyright © 2018 Tabbie Browne

All rights reserved, including the right to reproduce this book, or portions thereof in any form. No part of this text may be reproduced, transmitted, downloaded, decompiled, reverse engineered, or stored, in any form or introduced into any information storage and retrieval system, in any form or by any means, whether electronic or mechanical without the express written permission of the author.

This is a work of fiction. Names and characters are the product of the author's imagination and any resemblance to actual persons, living or dead, is entirely coincidental.

The views expressed in this work are solely those of the author and do not necessarily reflect the views of the publisher, and the publisher hereby disclaims any responsibility for them.

ISBN: 978-0-244-41502-0

PublishNation
www.publishnation.co.uk

A MESSAGE FROM THE AUTHOR

The author does not like or use the F word so it will not appear in any of her books. However, if you find there are many places in this novel where it would be very apt, please feel free to insert it at your pleasure.

Chapter 1

The air in the house was electric and almost crackled in anticipation of what was about to explode the minute the front door opened.

Maria's guardians were on full alert. They knew she was at breaking point and afraid that this time she may do something in anger that would ruin the rest of her earth life. She stood in the kitchen almost caressing her favourite carving knife, her lips set, for this time he would have to come up with a brilliant explanation, although she knew it would be lies.

There were five angels now trying to calm the surroundings but her frustration at being taken for a fool was brimming over and as soon as one area cooled another rose up. She was like a volcano that had to erupt.

At the sound of the key in the door, her head spun round and she grasped the knife as she slowly walked into the lounge.

"What's for dinner?" He called before breezing into the room but as soon as he saw her fixed gaze he stopped.

"Whatever you say, it will be lies." Maria's voice was very precise and every syllable cut through the air.

"Oh you're not going off on that one again? You're like a bloody record that's stuck."

Before she could answer he continued.

"Well then, if you're not going to believe me, there's no point in me keep telling you woman. You just think what you want if it keeps you happy. You're sick."

"Now you just shut up and listen to me Dixon." His real name was only used by his parents or to get his attention especially when his wife was annoyed. "I've put up with all I'm going to take from you. You don't even know what the truth is anymore. You live in your own little dream world and anyone who threatens to prick your bubble is the bad guy."

"Oh, so I can't enjoy life, I've got to sit here and jump through your hoops have I?" His eyes were flashing for although she was right, in his eyes she was being selfish.

The angels closed around her as they sensed her next move and as her arm came up the knife on full view she suddenly froze unable to take the next step. This was enough for Dick, with cries of how mad she was and wanted locking up he was out the door in a flash.

The air was calming as she felt herself guided to a chair and slowly lowered into the seat. As the danger was over, only two angels remained and the three left to go to other matters. Slowly Maria's soul was calmed into reasoning for her mind had almost been taken over with vengeance and a sense that justice must be done.

It was obvious this would only be a temporary measure because when someone has been trusted and betrays it, the victim usually feels that the record must be set straight at some point to restore the balance. They may not look at it so logically but that is what drives them.

The signs had been there, but often people don't want to believe it. Recently Maria had noticed various little changes in Dick's manner and he had stopped using some of the personal names they used. Also he could be a bit evasive if she started asking too many questions. He wasn't actually lying, but doing a fairly good job of avoiding the truth.

One of the guardians took a position next to the telephone, knowing it would be ringing in a moment while the other put soothing arms around the distraught woman. As expected, Maria jumped at the familiar tones and hesitated, wondering whether she could speak to anyone. Knowing who was calling, the nearest angel moved her to answer it.

"Hello."

"Is that you?"

The voice of her mother was comforting but it was sometimes irritating when she asked the same question and Maria was tempted to ask who else it could be but she held her tongue.

"Yes, are you all right?" She took the handset and sat in the nearest chair.

"Only you haven't been round, and there's no one to talk to."

"Mum I came round when I left work yesterday."

"Are you sure?"

"Yes Mum, you asked me to get you some kippers. Remember?"

There was silence for a moment so she continued.

"Mum, you haven't forgotten have you?"

"Well of course I haven't," then after a slight hesitation "are you sure that was yesterday, only I thought it was last week."

In truth she couldn't remember it at all but didn't want to admit it.

"Look I'm coming round tomorrow straight from work again." Maria was too weary for this just now but knew she had to support her mum and it was now she could have done with Dick's understanding rather than worrying who he was with all the time.

"I've not seen anyone today. Not a living soul." Beaty sighed.

"But Aunty Joan was coming."

Silence again for a moment.

"Oh? Well if she did I don't recall it."

Maria knew very well her mum's sister had been as they had arranged a rota between them. As they both worked it meant that neither of them had the pressure of going daily. They had realised recently that her condition was getting worse which was very sad as Beatrice, to use her correct name, had always been one to go round helping everyone else, whether they were sick or upset, she was there. But now there seemed to be no one to visit her except her immediate family which came down to the two of them.

Joan was seventy six, five years older than her sibling yet was still active and bright as a button. They were both widows and had been quite close until recent months when Beaty seemed to be coming more and more forgetful. She refused to have any medical help or examinations and it was obvious she was showing signs of early dementia although she wouldn't have agreed.

In a way the ladies felt they were coping with an in between state. The woman was neither confirmed to have the illness, nor acting normally.

"Did you hear me? You've gone very quiet."

Maria jumped as she realised her mum had been talking but hadn't any idea of what she had been saying.

"It's driving me that way too." She said aloud without thinking. "Oh sorry Mum, I missed the last bit."

"I said," slight pause to emphasise she was having to repeat herself "those sausages were off."

"But you didn't have sausages this week and they were bought fresh when you did." Maria sighed. She was weary but trying to hold it together.

"Well I'm sure you know best." The tone was mocking which was very hurtful to someone who had cared way beyond their duties.

"I will see you tomorrow as I said. Now don't forget."

Without even waiting for a reply she clicked the 'off' button and almost threw the phone down.

"What with her and him." Her head inclined towards the door. "I've had enough. What about me for a change?" And she dropped her head into her hands and cried partly from frustration and sadness for her mum and anger and resentment for the man who should be here right now not getting his end away with some useless slag.

Dick could never quite understand what all the fuss was about. He worked hard as a car mechanic, always paid his share towards the bills and saw no reason why he shouldn't go out and have his bit of 'fun' to relax. After all, Maria had her office job and liked to go out odd nights with one of her friends so what was her problem?

The difference, although he couldn't see it, was that on top of working and running the home, she was becoming more and more involved with her mother's welfare which, apart from the physical effort was also affecting her mental state. If anyone needed some chill time, it was her.

He had gone home hoping she would have a go at him, which gave him the perfect excuse to storm out and head off to his latest sex interest. He had no trouble finding plenty to suit his needs and vetted every female that came into the garage. Although he reckoned he was choosy, it didn't really matter to him what nationality they were, what age as long as they could still get into the right positions or even if they were married, engaged, in a relationship or single. If one finished with him, correction, if he finished with them there was always one in the wings waiting for her turn.

It wasn't far to the area where Cyn (she couldn't stand Cynthia) lived and as usual he parked a few yards away where there were no houses. She'd told him the neighbours were big time nosey and to be very careful coming and going. She was in her thirties, young enough to be his daughter. She did have two children from her failed marriage but for some reason that she kept to her self, they stayed with their gran a lot.

Having been on the look out since his phone call, the door was open ready for him to walk straight in. She opened her arms for a welcoming hug but after a mere quick embrace he pushed her aside and started to go upstairs.

"Where are you going? Desperate for a pee?" She called after him.

"No." He didn't turn round. "Well come on, I haven't got long."

With a disgruntled snort she slowly followed him and when she got to the landing she paused. He was already undressing and throwing his clothes on the floor at the side of the bed.

"What the hell do you think you're doing?" She almost screamed.

"What we normally do. Now stop farting about and get over here bitch."

"Hang on a minute, if you think you can walk in here without so much as a kiss my arse, you've got another think coming."

Before she had chance to say any more he had dragged her down and was forcing his tackle into her mouth.

The scream that emitted was priceless. Although he was too powerful for her to struggle against, she used the obvious weapon at her disposal. She sank her teeth into his equipment with such a force, he got off her and fell to the floor in agony. He was in too much pain to retaliate at the moment but she knew his temper would surface soon so she had to act quickly. Flying out of the room she went to the downstairs phone and called the police saying someone had come to her door, forced his way in and tried to rape her. It got a bit tricky when she had to explain it hadn't taken place just inside the house but upstairs but they assured her someone would be round as soon as possible.

The neighbours were indeed nosey and the commotion had attracted them from both sides. The ones adjoining had heard the scream as they happened to be in the upstairs room decorating, and when they came round to see if everything was alright, the ones on the other side wanted to know what was going on too. Cyn took this opportunity to have witnesses in case he came down and tried to attack her so kept them in conversation saying the police were coming. After that there was no way any of them were going anywhere and were soon joined by some from over the road.

Dick was trying to get to the bathroom to put some cold water on his injured bit to try and take some of the pain out of it and while he was grabbing the nearest flannel, he heard the noise from outside.

"Oh shit. Now what do I do?"

He couldn't very well go down the stairs cock in hand saying he'd been attacked, but how else could he get out. The pain was numbing his thinking but he started to panic. Struggling to open the bathroom window he tried to look out to see if he could make an escape that way, but there were no extensions to the building and it was a straight drop to the ground. Even if he risked it, how could he get out of the garden?

At that moment he thought he was hallucinating because he could see flashing lights but as he rubbed his eyes the truth hit him. They were blue. Before he could decide anything else he heard the tread on the stairs and turned to see two uniformed police staring at him.

The rest all happened so quickly and within minutes he was sitting in the back of the police car with one officer at the side of him while the other had dispersed the crowd and was talking to Cyn inside the house.

After a while the female pc came out and spoke to her partner.

Dick was left sitting in the car but wasn't going anywhere. A few moments later they opened the door and he was told that they thought he should go to hospital to have his wound checked out.

"I will. But she attacked me." He felt such a fool.

The male officer leaned down and said quietly,

"Whatever happened mate, we think this isn't the first time you've been here, in fact you are quite a regular visitor."

"What's she said?" Dick asked.

"Let's put it this way. You either came here as a stranger and tried to rape her, or…" he paused "you have both been having it off and it went a bit wrong tonight. Now which is it to be?"

Dick was quiet for a moment.

"Look officer, I'm a married man."

Both police looked at each other then the female went and brought Cyn to the car.

"Did he try to rape you?" She asked her.

"Well not exactly."

"Do you want to prefer charges or was it just your normal sex play?"

Cyn looked into the car, but he looked away.

"Not this time?" She whispered. "I think I've taught him a lesson."

"In which case we would suggest you keep it under control, or you will be done for wasting our time. Do you understand?" The female was not standing any messing.

To say Dick was relieved was an understatement but he still had to face Maria when he got home. He decided he didn't want to go to the hospital, in fact the least number of people seeing his injury the better.

When they were sure he was fit to drive, the male officer saw him to his car with a few choice man to man words of advice.

The female saw Cyn back indoors with a few bits of advice of her own.

All the excitement being over, the neighbours slowly dispersed but were soon on their phones the minute they got home.

The officers had a bit of a private giggle as they drove off, recalling many other similar cases.

If the air surrounding the house was filled with excitement regarding the recent happening it was nothing to the consternation going on in the unseen world. Dixon had two permanent guardians monitoring him who had been allocated way before his birth to his current life. In previous lives he had not only been wayward, pushing aside any help or guidance but directing his wrath against anything or anyone that threatened his way of existing. He was a prime example of a soul being controlled mainly by evil forces but that never stopped the good angels from constantly trying to veer him onto the right path and hopefully eventually lead the life of a good person. But his time was running out. He had used up most of his earth lives and this was the last one allocated to him so if the good powers couldn't wrench him free this time, they stood little chance of ever achieving their goal, which to them was a failure. Of course they knew the strength of the evil they were fighting but their optimism always drove them towards the target of one hundred percent success, which was impossible but they never lowered their objectives.

His two regular guardians were with him as he drove home. The signal had already gone to those protecting Maria as they all knew there would be fireworks the minute he entered the house.

He parked the car and got out, the pain in his willy still intense. Slowly he went to the front door and fumbled for his key. He found the lock and pushed it in. It wouldn't turn. Frantically he tried again and again and just when he was about to hammer on the door he heard the noise of the lock being undone and the door slowly opened a few inches.

"Yes?" Maria's voice was curt.

"Let me in you idiot,"

"Excuse me? What was that again?"

"I said, let me in." The last works were almost screamed.

"Oh, thrown you out has she? What a pity."

The flow of profanities that followed did him no good for the door was slammed in his face.

The noise was attracting attention and a couple of the neighbours came out to see what was going on. Maria appeared at the bedroom window which she flung open and leaned out looking down on him.

"You ok love?" One man called.

She looked in the direction of the voice.

"Yes I'm good ta Bill."

"Need any help?" Bill wasn't a small man by any stretch of the imagination and he tended to use his muscle before his brain so he wasn't one to mess with.

"Well," Maria indicated to the doorstep, "something seems to have been dumped by the door."

All the neighbours knew of Dick's philandering and many felt sorry for his wife as she had always been a good person and didn't deserve the likes of him. She would always help anyone with a problem and put herself out where most wouldn't have bothered. They all agreed she needed a good man, not this lump of garbage.

"Oh I can soon clear that for you love."

As he started to stride towards the house his wife warned him not to get too involved or he might be the one in trouble.

"It's ok Bill," Maria answered "but I suppose the prat had better be inside before there's any further agro."

"Well if you're sure." Was the reply much to the relief of his wife.

Maria looked back to her doorstep.

"Wait there." She called.

"How the hell can I do anything else?" Dick yelled.

She was in charge now.

"Oh well if you're going to be shitty about it, you can stay there all night for all I care."

"No, wait. I've been injured."

This made the neighbours stop and move a bit closer. This was getting good now. Where had he been injured? They had to know even if it was so that they could be the first to pass it on to their friends.

"Let's have a look." One called out much to the amusement of the others.

"Has she chopped your dick off Dick?" Another added.

"Nah. Not enough blood. It pours out I've heard." Bill said.

The sound of the door opening brought a hush to the assembly.

"You'd better get your disgusting carcass in here." Maria framed the doorway. "We'll be having the press here next."

As he limped in, the onlookers started a slow hand clap in time to his movements and when the door had shut behind the pair, everyone started to drift back to their own homes, with comments flitting between them.

"Ha, wouldn't be in his shoes."

"Wouldn't want to be in his bed."

"I feel sorry for her."
"Oh yeah, I do."
"I'd have thrown him out long ago."
"She's too good for the likes of him."
"Scum bag."
"Arse wipe."

Although these remarks couldn't be heard from inside the house, Maria could only guess as to what people would be saying and even that was getting to her. She knew they meant well but you couldn't stop gossip and by the morning everyone in the area would know, whether it was the truth or not for some would have to elaborate to make a better story.

Maria's guardian spirits had already made sure there was plenty of back up for the confrontation and when the woman had slowly opened the door for her husband to enter, they were giving her all the strength and protection possible. Some were calming the atmosphere in the house to try and dampen the pent up emotions which were permeating everything.

Dick's guardians were also keen to keep everything at low key but they were at a disadvantage, for the evil pranksters which had been attached to this man's soul for decades, refused to release their hold and as soon as the good forces took control, they zoomed in and undid all that had been achieved. This, being an old fight it showed no signs of abating while this man was in earthly form, or even totally in spirit.

Anyone in tune with the spirit world would have felt the tension and while to the novice onlooker it may have appeared that all was quiet, it was far from the truth.

Just as Maria was indicating Dick to a chair, but keeping her distance, the phone rang.

"Oh buggar!" It slipped out before she had time to check her words. "That'll be Mum again."

She pointed a finger at him and said very sternly "Sit there for a minute and don't move."

She grabbed the handset and spoke still watching him.

"Yes Mum, what is it now?"

There was silence for a moment then she turned away from him and said in a quieter voice "Sorry, thought it would be Mum again."

Dick was eyeing her rather suspiciously and if his tackle hadn't hurt so much he would have grabbed the phone from her. If he could have heard the conversation, it would have been thrown across the room in anger, whereas he had no option but to sit and wait, his whole body throbbing.

By coincidence, one of Maria's friends, Amy had just had a call from her mum who happened to live across the road from Cyn.

"I didn't like to say but thought you'd rather hear it from me before it gets out like."

Without giving anything away Maria simply said "Go on."

"Well, me Mam saw these blue lights see, and it was a police car outside that woman that, well has a lot of blokes round."

There was a pause and as Maria didn't speak, Amy carried on.

"Well, they took this bloke, one that had been in the house, and put him in the police car, and the woman cop went back in and was talking to the slut. Anyway after a time they let him go but there was no car there, at her house I mean."

Maria was almost afraid to think what was coming next. Still she remained silent.

Amy was in full swing.

"Now then, me Mam's friend who lives a bit further down saw this bloke, not walking very well but going off down that bit where there's no houses. So what does she do but grabs her dog's lead and takes it for a walk to have a nose about and ..." she paused either for effect or because she was wary about the next bit, ".....now this is the funny thing."

"Go on." Maria said calmly.

"Well, she'd seen it before and when she told me Mam, well she said she was certain it was your Dick's car."

"It's ok. Thank you," she was about to say 'Amy' but hesitated and decided not to use a name, "much appreciated."

"You know if there's anything I can do." Amy wasn't letting go in the hopes of grabbing a bit more gossip but Maria wasn't going there.

She hung up and looked across to her husband.

"Who was that?" He almost snapped.

"Never mind." She smirked now. "I suppose you're going to say you got bitten by a dog?"

Was this a chance to get out of the truth or was she playing with him? She'd done it before and could be quite vicious when annoyed. What did bother him was she appeared to be too calm and very calculated.

"Doesn't matter what or how. I'm in agony. Isn't that all that matters?"

"Well," she said pushing up her sleeves, "we'd better have a look hadn't we?"

Panic now set in. She would know at once that they were teeth marks and not inflicted by a dog.

Chapter 2

Beaty was fumbling with the phone. Sadly she thought she could still pick up one of the old handsets with the large earpiece and an equally big bit you could speak into. She had been struggling with the modern sort and so Maria had also put one in that was plugged in and she felt a bit happier with that. This rather defeated the object of having something with her in case she needed help or had a fall, but her mind was set and it was more to bother with.

While she was looking for Joan's number, the phone rang and she nearly dropped it.

"Yes, who's that?" She said warily when she finally put it to her ear.

"It's me, Joan."

"Who?"

"Beaty, it's your sister Joan. Joan." She repeated when there was nothing but silence.

"Joan? Well alright but there's no need to shout, I'm not deaf."

"You didn't answer and I didn't know if you were there."

Beaty gave a snort.

"Well of course I'm here, how else could I be speaking to you? You know Joan sometimes I wonder if you know what's going on."

Her sister took a deep breath before she said, as calmly as she could "How are you.?"

"Who, me? I'm alright, are you?"

"Yes, I'm fine thank you. Now did you remember to eat the dinner I brought you?"

There was a pause because obviously the poor thing couldn't recall it.

"Just a minute." Beaty said and Joan knew she had put the phone on the table and gone off to check.

After a few moments the reply came back.

"Yes it was lovely, very nice."

This was going to be tricky.

"Beaty, are you sure you ate it, only you do forget a bit lately."

There was the definite sound of a huff.

"Well the plate's been washed up and it's on the side ready for you." The tone was curt.

"You know I'm only looking out for your welfare, so is Maria. We just need to know you are ok." Joan was feeling very weary but tried to sound kind and loving.

"Yes, you are both very good to me."

Just as Joan was about to ring off, her sister started telling her about one of her neighbours as though there was no problem at all.

"And you should have seen her leg. They said it was a funny colour and dripping all over the place. Well that can't be right can it? Something should be done about it."

"So did you go round?" Joan asked.

"Me? No, I wouldn't go there. Her daughter told me about it. Sounds horrible doesn't it?"

Stifling a yawn Joan agreed and said she'd ring her later to make sure she was ok for bed.

Beaty looked at the receiver in her hand, then to the phone before deciding she had to put one back onto the other.

"Hmm. People, never got any time these days." She muttered to herself as she sat back in her armchair. Her eyes closed and she fell fast asleep.

The two guardians watched as she drifted and as she slowly left her physical state she greeted them, recognising her resident angel Sofia.

"Got company? Is it busy tonight?" Her spiritual side had no problem with memory and she transformed into an entirely different person to the one her sister had spoken to.

"There's quite a bit of activity round here for some reason."

They beckoned her to place herself between them as they drifted up.

"It's such a tremendous relief to be out of that body." She would have whispered but all the communication was purely in thought.

"You looked ready for some light relief." Was the reply.

"If it's what I saw last time, it won't be light." Beaty was remembering witnessing one of the many quarrels between Maria and Dick.

"It's not just them. There's plenty of other similar cases going on, in fact its spreading like a virus. And you don't have to be in on this one."

"No No." Beaty was insistent. "It's my way of doing what I can to keep her as safe as possible. And I mean from herself and what she might do."

They were all aware that in her waking time Beaty would have no knowledge of her spiritual work, but the results they had achieved on numerous occasions proved to be of enormous benefit resulting in Maria being prevented from doing anything detrimental or even illegal.

"I wouldn't have liked to be on the end of that knife." The assistant angel said.

Beaty reacted. "Oh, come to that has it?" Then added "She didn't…."

"No." Sofia cut in. "Not yet."

"Is that where we are going now?" The assistant asked.

"No, going to have a look at something else first."

And with that they immediately took their positions over their prime target.

Sofia indicated the house that Dick had just left. They had been here before so Beaty was aware it was one of his regular haunts, for the time being anyway. It wouldn't last long for he'd either be dumped or leave this one for another. Quite often there wasn't only one on the go.

"Are you ready for this?" The Sofia asked without expecting a reply.

As if on cue a woman came scurrying up the road and as soon as she was at the front door tapped quietly but urgently. As soon as it opened she hurried inside.

Beaty took a close look.

"Isn't that?" She didn't finish the question.

"Its Amy, Maria's friend." The assistant answered. "Quite a regular little visitor."

"At all times, day or night." Then Sofia added. "She rang Maria to tell her what had gone on tonight, just as a good friend of course."

"But didn't add that she's often more than an observer." The other added.

Beaty was fuming.

"And he's always saying 'I'm not going anywhere, I'll never leave you' to her. Well I wish he would. What he doesn't add is that he will stay with her but have every bit on the side that's free. I take it he isn't paying for it."

"Well if the police have their eye on it and they know there's two women working it, it's a brothel." The two angels agreed.

"I don't care what he does, I just want him out of her life." Beaty was determined and wouldn't give up until this had been achieved.

They watched from inside the house for a while. The main activity from the women was trawling through social media throwing out the net for the next fish. It was obvious the surrounding area was filled with all sorts of entities ready to catch a free ride for excitement, some of them even putting candidates in their path. When anyone was being entertained, the unseen audience had a field day satisfying their own desires which many hadn't experienced when in body. It was as if they had to make up for lost time and get a certain amount of points to be able to move on to higher and more intense satisfaction.

People who accept the physical as being the only plane, little know what danger they attract and much of it can then hook on to affect their spiritual development. This makes the good angels' work so much more difficult, for if you tried to explain to these folk what was going on they wouldn't want to listen, until of course, when it would be too late.

Cyn and Amy were already on this path and there were plenty of elements ready to seize them for their own uses. Dick's association with not only these women but others like them, meant he was already on a downhill run with his foot on the gas.

The three spirits having observed all they needed for now then set off to their other tasks.

Beaty was keen to check on Maria as she knew things were about to blow in that household. Sofia was a bit wary as she knew having a personal interest could affect her actions, also her daughter had her own guardians to protect her. However they decided a quick visit wouldn't go amiss and in a split second were hovering over the bathroom where the couple were now concentrating on Dick's wound. There were only two good spirits in presence for Maria but there seemed to have been an invitation sent out for all the non desirables to come and witness the injury. Some were highly delighted and enjoying the view but others had more sinister reasons. A small evil gang had joined but not for gratification, because they thrived on revenge and here was a perfect case for a man to get even with his wife. They soon picked up the fact that she was going to enjoy inflicting more pain in the pretence of caring for him.

Beaty and her companion recognised this visiting element immediately and although the remaining spirits would be aware of the presence they may not realise their sadistic intentions.

It was too early to call for back up but the message soon went to higher levels to be on the alert as evil factions were hovering, their intentions being far from benevolent. This would not be an isolated case. If they were active, they would seek out any situation in the area and insert their evil into any willing host. The targets wouldn't realise they were being selected and any resulting outcome would be put down to their own talents, whereas they would simply be tools in the hands of sadistic manipulators. The persons used would appear to be either at an all time low and need help from any kind soul they could use, or would have the right chat up lines to extort, injure or simply drive their subjects insane. It wouldn't be until it was too late that the poor victim would realise just how blind they had been. Everyone else would see it, and if a kind or observant friend or relative pointed it out, they would be ignored.

So what had started out as a bit on the side, had now drawn Dick into something which could be terrifying not only for him, but for his innocent and long suffering wife.

Joan had become very restless of late. She knew her sister was entering the realm of dementia, it was too obvious, but the problem was going to be how to get her diagnosed. She wouldn't even talk about it and fobbed it off as though Joan was making it up. Fortunately, with Maria being equally aware, it did mean they could at least share the burden.

As she sat having a cup of tea, her mind drifted to her niece. She'd always liked her, she was a happy child and grew up always thinking of other people. But when she met Dixon, Joan knew from the start it was doomed. She could see beneath his happy exterior that this was someone not to be trusted. He gave the impression he would do anything for anybody at anytime. Just ask and he would be there. His media posts were full of how he cared for others, but behind that façade was a self centred, mean uncaring individual.

When once they were married, Maria soon learned of her mistake, but none of his true self had been noticeable while they were courting so she had no reason to believe he would change so drastically. He'd shown no interest in their three children from birth and as soon as the first one was on the way he started his extra marital relationships. For a few years he managed to keep them quiet, always making excuses for going out and with Maria tied up with looking after the little ones, she failed to notice. It was only when he seemed to be going out at the same time on certain days that it started to register. The children were all of school age and she thought she might take a part time job to help with them having a holiday.

At first it was just a hunch then she started to take mental note of his comings and goings. Then she overheard a conversation in the supermarket and realised it was Dick they were talking about.

When she confronted him, his attitude was that he worked hard so he would play hard. He didn't deny anything and just shrugged it off. If she persisted he started with the familiar "Oh I mustn't have any pleasure. Why does everyone always blame me?" She accused him of being totally selfish and only thinking of himself to which he just smiled.

From then on their marriage was a disaster but she hadn't the means to walk out or she would have done with no hesitation whatsoever.

So now she was looking down at his love tackle with a satisfied smirk on her face.

"I don't know why I'm doing this?" She had some cotton wool in one hand and a bottle of rather strong antiseptic in the other. "I mean, you should have got it treated where you did it."

She leaned forward. "Hmm that does look as though it could get infected if you ask me."

"Well I'm not bloody well asking you, now are you going to put that damned stuff on or not?"

"Just a minute," she put everything on the shelf, "I'd better get some gloves, just to be safe you know, wouldn't want to catch anything contagious."

"For Christ's sake hurry it up, I'm dying here."

"Oh dear." She said over her shoulder as she reached for some plastic gloves in the drawer.

Pulling them on slowly she reached for the bottle.

"What the hell are you doing?" His hand went over his injury. You've forgotten the cotton wool."

"Nope." She smirked inches from his face. "With a bite like that it needs hands on treatment. Oh listen to me, I should have said teeth."

With that she tipped the antiseptic straight onto his willy.

The yell that went up was priceless.

The onlookers were split into three groups. His guardians were trying to calm the atmosphere and protect him as one group was having the best entertainment they could have wished for, almost jumping up and down at the screams and cheering him on. But the evil entities were out for revenge. They would use him to direct his own hatred against this woman who thought herself so clever, so smug. But she would soon learn that you don't mess with their kind.

With Dixon being temporarily out of the running, Cyn and Amy were eager to fill his 'slot'. They had their regulars but were always on the look out for something new.

"He was getting boring." Cyn mused as they flicked through some on line hopefuls.

"Already got more like." Amy was looking at the screen as her friend scrolled. "He looks fit."

"Nah. Desperate more like." Cyn pulled a face. "And we aren't."

Amy thought for a moment.

"We aren't what?"

Things often had to be explained which sort of took the edge off the statement and a joke often lost its punch. Ignoring the remark Cyn carried on searching.

"We aren't what?" Amy repeated.

"What you on about? We're supposed to be looking, unless you don't want that extra bit of earnings."

"But I don't know what you meant."

"Look just forget it, The moment's gone. OK?"

Amy huffed. Sometimes other people spoke too quickly or said things she didn't understand but they never seemed to want to explain. Still feeling a bit peeved she watched for a while then got up and stood over Cyn.

"Anyway, you always give me the horrible ones while you have the scrummy ones."

It was Cyn's turn to sigh. She slapped both hands on the table, pushed the laptop to one side and stood to face her.

"What's your bleat?"

"Um, what I said then." Amy was lost when faced with someone as strong willed as this woman.

"If you don't like it lady, you can do one. I'm ok without the likes of you, and anyway....."

"What do you mean? Anyway."

"Oh my god. Do I have to spell it out. Yes I expect I frigging well do." Cyn was getting frustrated and angry with this wet rag.

"Look, and try and take this in if you can. Some of our male visitors, like a bit of, shall we say class. They haven't come here for a quick jump and off."

"Some do." Amy was pouting.

Cyn looked her straight in the eye.

"And they are the ones you can cope with. In, out, goodnight."

"But they like me."

"Oh give me bloody strength. They aren't here to like you, they come for a lay. Get it. There's no affection in it. They just want to shoot their load."

Amy's mouth was open.

"But they aren't all like it."

"Oh go and read the manual." As soon as the words left Cyn's mouth she could have bitten her tongue out for it was obvious what was coming next.

"Manual? I didn't know……."

"Never mind. Now are you in or out? Because I'm not wasting any more time on you. With all you do I could handle the lot myself, in more ways than one I can tell you."

Most people would have either slapped her, punched her or given her a tirade of colourful abuse, but Amy hadn't a clue. Without Cyn she would be lost. She sat down slowly.

"I was never good at anything."

"Oh don't give me that sob story again. I've tried haven't I? I've worked my tits off but you just don't seem to take it in. It's a basic instinct, shagging, animals do it without being taught."

"But I can do it."

Cyn gave the biggest sigh she could. You had to almost feel sorry for this creature but why did she have to be in her stable?

"Yes dear. Anybody can lie there with their legs open but there's more to it than that. It's an art. You've got to know what is where and the effect it has when you handle it right."

The blank stare said it all.

Cyn couldn't resist the next bit.

"I don't suppose you even know where all your bits are."

"What?"

By this time, some of the evil element at Dick's had picked up the connection and were in presence during the women's conversation and realised that here was a foothold. They had two angles, one the experienced woman who was always looking for that extra bit of excitement and something new, and the one brain cell who would be so easily led, she would be putty in their grip. This kind of situation lent itself to ongoing control.

Cyn's mode was to let the men have the first visit completely free but whet their appetite so much they had to go back, then they were only too willing to pay. But men or women who chase this kind of pleasure are so wrapped up in their own enjoyment it can become a drug and they give no thought to the consequences should the lid come off. This is where the likes of Cyn have a hold, because if a good client threatens to leave, she only has to suggest that the person could be exposed to keep them in her web. But what she doesn't realise if that she is feeding the evil element with much more sinister consequences. For it isn't only the earthly life which is affected, it can have far reaching effects on the existence of the soul. The evil are constantly reeling in the catch and have no intention of letting them ever escape.

The likes of Cyn and Amy may appear to be small fry, but connections are strange things. A fairly unknown individual may come on the scene but could have friends in high places who think that getting their relief away from the normal circuit would be completely safe and they would never be detected. Although money maybe no object, some could be pretty mean when it came to parting with their own cash and small amounts wouldn't have to be explained to any partners.

So here was a good spot to concentrate on and if it ruined lives so much the better.

Dixon was in bed. His groin was throbbing but not for the usual reasons. He was sure his wife had damaged him even more and he should have some sort of medical attention but how could he do that?

"Take this bloody dressing off." He yelled as Maria came back into the room.

"No No, you need that on in case of infection."

She smirked as she lifted the sheet to reveal the biggest bandage imaginable. She'd really gone to town with it and when he objected she simply gave it a sharp tap which brought more howls of agony. She was going to milk this.

"You see it's very difficult with it not being as hard as it was when you got bitten, I can't see the full extent of the wound where you got bitten, but if it had been down, when you got bitten......"

"Shut up, shut up, shut up." He screamed. "Why do you have to keep rubbing it in?"

"Oh you want me to rub it in a bit more!" She moved to touch it.

He now went berserk trying to rip off the dressing but she had taped it so much the more he pulled the worse mess it made.

"Get this bloody thing off." He yelled.

"Oh dear is it bleeding now, where you got ……."

"You say that once more and I'll……."

"You'll do what?"

For the first time he noticed she had the big kitchen knife in her other hand and she was waving it to and fro very slowly. Panic set in now.

"What….what are you doing with that?" He was becoming hysterical.

She gave the most sadistic smile he had ever seen.

"Let me see now, I really ought to dig the bite out, oh silly me, it wasn't a bee sting was it? No I think there is only one thing I can do then your cock won't hurt any more, because you won't have one."

The last few words were shouted so loud the neighbours must have heard.

Maria's main guardian had sent out the signal for help and Sofia and Beaty were there instantly. While mum put a protective restrain around her daughter, the others formed a shield so that no further connection could be made between them. Although Dick's good angels were doing their best the other two elements were still in presence and some were goading Maria to carry on and finish the job. The most evil ones were building up the hatred in Dick himself, so that if he didn't get the better of her this time due to his current state, it would fester and later he would implement his full revenge on her.

Chapter 3

So that she didn't get stagnant and let life drift by, Joan did some voluntary work at a local charity shop. She could still do her share in looking out for her sister but she felt she needed a bit of purpose and something to get her out of the house. There were quite a variety of people that frequented the place, some regulars, some just passing by and the little band of helpers who came in on certain days. She was happy to work with all ages and had become quite friendly with Evie, one of the younger ones who had taken to her because she wasn't 'geriatric' as she called it.

"We used to say fuddy duddy when I was young." Joan would laugh.

"Don't you worry, I'll get you with it. You're not like the others." She'd say.

Evie was eighteen and went to the local uni but felt she wanted experience with life in general. Her mum had always taught her to do something to help others so this seemed perfect and she could fit it in round her studies. She told Joan she'd teach her how to use a laptop.

"That's a computer, but that's about all I know about it." Joan had laughed.

It was the day after the 'biting' and word hadn't seeped through yet. When the phone rang in the shop Joan answered.

"He did what?"

Evie looked up and Joan beckoned her over, putting her finger to her mouth to be quiet.

"But are you alright?" Joan was intent on finding out what had gone on.

Evie was inclining to try and hear.

"Do you want me to come round? Oh you're at work, well will he manage on his own?"

Obviously Maria had assured her there was nothing she could do.

"Well alright dear, I'll see you later. Bye."

She put the phone down, looked at the younger woman and said "Well!"

"What's gone on?" Evie wanted to know everything as it sounded a bit choice.

"It's my niece's husband, only you mustn't say anything. But someone's bitten his privates."

The hoot that went up made Joan smile.

"What, love bitten his cock?"

"Well, in a manner of speaking, I mean I don't know the details."

"Oh I wish someone had put a pic on social." Evie felt lost if nothing was posted for all to see. She grabbed her phone and started tapping around to see if she could find anything.

"Well like I say, I don't quite know what happened. But I shouldn't think it was at home." Joan gave a little cough.

Evie was laughing.

"You know that happened to my friend's boyfriend. Ever so embarrassing it was. We all called him hicky dicky."

The similarity of the name brought Joan down to earth. What had really happened? His philanderings were no secret and she felt for Maria because she would get the flack of the gossip. If only she could leave him.

"Well what do you think? Shall I?" Evie's questions brought her out if her thoughts.

"I'm sorry. I was miles away."

"There's this really nice bloke I've been talking to only he's a bit too old for me, and I was wondering if you'd like to meet him?"

"What? I mean, me meet a man?" This wasn't what Joan was expecting and although the girl meant well she would have to make it clear that she wasn't looking for anybody.

"Just as a friend, unless of course you want to take it further."

"I'm alright I think, but thank you anyway."

Evie gave her a look which said that she wasn't giving up on this one but Joan was more concerned about Maria at the moment. As far as her rotten husband was concerned, his thing could drop off for all she cared. Might be a blessing to society.

She couldn't help thinking of how lucky she had been to have such a wonderful husband. He was thoughtful, loving and always put her first, but he was no wimp, he had worked hard and provided for their needs and above all had been true to her. They had really looked forward to retirement when they would do all the things they planned but sadly he had suddenly been taken ill about twelve months before he was due to finish and had died in a very short space of time. She had never looked at anyone since and had no wish to get into any sort of relationship because she would always be comparing them to him and nobody could come up to him.

Evie looked up from her phone and tossed it into her bag.
"Well I'm not saying it would be long term, you know, just a friendship wouldn't hurt."
"Pardon, sorry I was just thinking......."
"No it's ok, but if someone nice did happen to come from, oh I don't know, maybe just come into here, what I'm saying is there's no harm in having a friend to go for a drink, movies, you know, a companion."
Joan didn't want to nurture this conversation so she started fiddling with things on the counter without looking up.
"Yes, well we'll see."
She thought she had better give a neutral reply or the girl would have been like a dog with a bone and she rather hoped she would forget all about it.
Her mind turned back to Maria. She needed to talk to her alone. Maybe she would suggest they both went to Beaty's for a change, then they would have chance to speak without him listening. Of course she wanted to now what had actually happened although it was fairly clear, but she was more bothered about her niece and the effect this could have.

Dick crawled out of bed closely observed by the growing audience in the spirit world. Due to the interest from the evil sector, his good angels had upped their support, not because of the mischievous ones, they could cope with them, but the more sinister band which seemed to be waiting in the wings ready to pounce.
He went to the bathroom and cursed the dressings Maria had insisted he have. Every time he'd needed a pee, she had slowly removed them and then put them back afterwards and he swore she

had put more on each time. Well this time they weren't going back. As he tried to unwind the bandage he realised she had taped it underneath where he couldn't see. Desperately he tried pulling at it which only made a bigger mess of things. As his bladder was reaching bursting point he grabbed pair of scissors and tried to make a hole in the end so at least he could wee through that which worked but in his panic the inevitable happened. As he clumsily tried to cut the bandage, he also snipped his knob, so here he was, yelling with pain at the new injury, trying to aim for the bowl and his temper exploding. There is no need to list the profanities.

The unseen world around him was a hive of activity. His guardians were doing their best to calm him and even trying and ease the pain but the mischievous gang were having a field day. This group of ugly, sadistic morons weren't going to let this entertainment go by without milking it and were goading him on, trying to make him so angry his only relief would be utter revenge. But the higher ranking evil had other plans and when the time came, the lower scum would be despatched. But they were a good distraction for now so let them have their day.

The higher levels of angels knew the sort of tricks the demons used but were always on the alert for anything new. The guardians at the scene were only updated as the hierarchy deemed fit, as they knew the evil could hack into them and always be one step ahead. So the good powers had to be just as conniving.

Having finally exposed his bits to the air, Dick first filled the bowl and tried to dangle everything into the soothing water but had to splash himself to achieve anything. Even with bragging there was no way he would have got it anywhere near the surface. At first he jumped and yelled again but slowly it seemed to give him some relief and the antiseptic didn't seem to have left any rash or the burns he expected. He reached for a mirror to examine the extent of his injuries underneath. All seemed fine so the problem was confined to his fireman's helmet. He could make out the teeth marks although the skin didn't seem to be broken and the scissors had only left a small scratch which had bled a bit but for the first time he realised just how much Maria had overplayed this.

He should have been at work by now and rang the garage to say he'd had a stomach upset but would been in later.

"Yes we know!" The mechanic said on the other end of the phone and the chuckles were there in the background.

"What do you mean, you know?"

"Oh well," it was obvious the word had spread, "perhaps you should take 'em out for a meal, not leave 'em that hungry."

"Look I don't know what you've heard but……"

"Just get your arse in here oh and don't forget to put some protection on it, wouldn't want you to get it infected, well not here anyway."

Dick slammed the phone down. How was he going to face that lot now? Then his ego started to return.

"Hey, I'm a stud. It's all jealousy, just 'cause they can't get their ends away. I'll show 'em."

If ever a man changed so quickly, he did. In minutes he'd grabbed a couple of biscuits, had a quick swig of the cold tea Maria had left and was out of the door.

"Right, let's see who's the bloody fool now."

He got in his car and drove quicker than he should to face the jeering idiots.

Beaty was back in body which meant she had no recollection of her spiritual activities. Had she been of a higher level, she could have combined the two continuously but at her stage sadly the physical illness deprived her of any recognition in her waking hours. In practical terms, it would be a blessing when she could throw off her mortal trappings and work solely in spirit but to those left it would always be a loss.

She couldn't remember if she had made anything for breakfast. As she sat in her chair she asked herself if she felt hungry but as she didn't she must have had something.

"I wonder what the enemy says."

She looked at the clock on the mantelpiece.

"Oh half past nine." She pondered for a moment. "Is that morning or night, because if it's night I ought to be getting ready for bed."

Then she noticed the sun shining on the garden.

"Perhaps it is morning."
She looked out of the window to see if anyone was going by.
"I wonder what day it is."
She didn't have a paper anymore as she couldn't be bothered to read it as, according to her it was always full of rubbish and not worth the money. It didn't occur to her to put the television on as that would have given her a clue.
"I'd like to go out." She decided. "But I haven't got anywhere to go."

Her angel stayed close as this was a dangerous time. When someone's mind is affected by illness, accident or disease it can act as a beacon for bad forces to attack. Although the person doesn't realise it, the turmoil in their mind is often activated by such horrible beings, such as those who delight in creating uncertainly, confusion and general unrest which is why someone often sits there and just cries for no reason. It is often put down to frustration which in a way is true because they are being shown what they used to be like and what they are now. Almost ramming in their faces but showing them that it has all gone and they will never experience it again.

Sometimes the angels will bring a family member to give comfort but this can be double edged. For some it will be great comfort knowing their loved one is still with them and will always be, but for others they feel the tremendous loss and can't wait to join them. So in that case the relative or friend is withdrawn, not only for the person still in body but to save the one totally in spirit from added distress. One can only imagine what it must be like to watch your relative grieving and your arms go out to comfort them but their sadness blocks the contact. You can beg them to open their mind to let you get close, but it can only come from them and hopefully someone to give them the right advice.

As he drove to work, Dick's mind wasn't, as you would expect, on the recent happenings and giving his joystick a rest for a while, but on who the next candidate would be. There were a few possibilities but he was getting a bit tired of some of the low life he'd had recently and felt he was worth more. So when he had parked the car he strolled into the workshop quite casually with a smug expression on his face.

One or two looked up with a smirk and it wasn't long before the comments were being bandied about.

"Did he leave a bit in?"

"Depends on how much got wopped off."

"Will it grow back?"

Dick grabbed his overalls, checked there were no customers on the premises and announced in a loud voice "Ok you've had your fun you wankers, and for your information I'm not lacking anything anywhere. You're all just jealous."

"Hope you'd had your jabs though." Was just loud enough to be heard.

Before he could throw a jibe it was followed by "And her!"

The foreman was all for a bit of fun but couldn't let this get out of hand so immediately send Dick of to do an MOT and wagged his finger at the rest of them indicating enough was enough, but couldn't resist a smirk of his own as he went into the little office.

As he worked, Dick's mind was sifting through all the women he had come across lately. Obviously he would steer clear of Cyn's area but he seemed to recall a tasty piece that lived on the opposite side of town. That might be worth a bit of homework, as soon as his soreness had worn off of course, because it wouldn't be a good introduction to flash teeth marks at a new conquest.

How quickly one can be back on form when it suits them.

Regardless of who's night it was for a visit, Joan and Maria decided that tonight they would go to Beaty's together. Obviously Joan was keen to hear in private what had gone on but they felt that to keep their own sanity, and with each other's company they would cope better as the condition worsened. It was easy to talk when they were making the bed, or washing up as Beaty would sit in her chair sometimes forgetting they were there. There was also the fact that she seem to be coming slightly incontinent, and although it wasn't too much of a problem right now, it would be before long.

They were chatting on the phone as Maria left work.

"I mean we could do odd nights on our own so that we each get a bit of a break," Joan was saying "think it would be good for both of us, that would."

"Sounds good to me." Maria paused then said "We've just got to get her checked out, but how?"

"Ah now you've said what I've be thinking."

"She won't have it you know."

Joan sighed.

"I know. But hang on. There's a chap comes in the shop that I think works with that kind of thing. Now what's his name? Oh I know, it's Frank. I could have a word with him if you like. His number's behind the desk because he's a lot to do with the elderly and the like."

"What we got to loose?" Maria was feeling drained so anything sounded good at the moment.

Agreeing to see each other soon, they rang off and Maria found herself slowing as she made her way home. What on earth was going to meet her this time?

Amy did a couple of cleaning jobs to keep some money coming in to pay the essential bills but it wasn't enough for any extras so when she learned that she could earn easy money she had jumped at it. Although Cyn found her the work, she was becoming a bit peeved that she never got the choice of who she would end up with. After a while she realised that what Cyn was charging the men wasn't what was passed on to her and she had done the work. But, as was pointed out in no uncertain terms, where would she be without someone to lead and provide the quality. The alternative was to take a kerb crawler up some alley, bang bang, pay up and off. Of course Cyn didn't want to loose her because this was easy money for her while she was taking her cut. But she felt she took all the risks so she deserved it.

It wasn't one of her evening cleaning nights so Amy sat fiddling with a strand of her hair expecting a call to say she was required.

"Sod her and sod them." She looked far from attractive when she was in one of her moods and not many clients would have chosen her unless that's all that was on offer.

"Why should I be her tool? I don't have to have what she picks for me. And she always keeps the best for herself."

The television was on although she wasn't really watching it until suddenly an advert came on for a dating site. She leaned forward.

"Now that's it!" She clapped her hands together. "I could go on one of those and get my own chaps."

She scrambled about trying to find a pen and something to write on but by the time she had both in front of her, the ad was long finished. But that didn't matter. Now she sat and thought for a moment. Didn't one of the women at the morning job tell her that you could go on line for this kind of stuff. For boyfriends, friends all sorts. That was it. Then she wouldn't need 'madam do dah', then she'd show her and make her jealous.

"And you can come crawling to me you prossie, hey you could even work for me."

She hadn't thought it all through of course. Where she would operate for a start. In this pokey tatty place? It may have been in the same area as Cyn, but there the similarity ended. She didn't have the finesse to demand big money or the experience to put it into practice. She'd had straightforward sex plenty of times but never varied it and when she'd been asked to do particular things, even nature hadn't given her the intelligence to know what half of the blokes were on about.

Her thought waves were attracting the unsavoury element who knew this would provide not only great entertainment but they could get her in their power and then send her out to perform on their orders. A perfect target.

If Cyn had been privy to the woman's intentions she may have been pleased to get her off her back but for the time being the extra she could earn from her wasn't to be fobbed off lightly. The same element was also taking root in her abode for some certain evil cells wallowed in the physical happenings as opposed to the spiritual ones and they had an exceedingly strong influence over their subjects. As is usual in these cases, the earthlings think they are running the show whereas they are simply being manipulated for the gratification of beings that have the power to affect their future spiritual development and even destroy their soul for eternity. Hence the danger that was threatening this area. It was time to bring in more powerful good angels before it was too late.

Sofia had requested backup to keep a general eye on the area around the two women for although it was highly unlikely that Dick would frequent the place for some time, attachments can be made through contacts.

It doesn't always have to be a physical encounter. Simply talking to someone on the phone is enough and the longer the call, the more interest is nurtured. Therefore if two people talk to each other for an hour or so every day, the elements treat this as a serious connection. But nowadays what earthlings don't realise is that all kind of media especially social, are making connections like multiple spiders webs so that once the trail is laid it is permanent. Whenever anyone has spoken to anyone face to face, phoned, written to, chatted on line or communicated by any means, the link is there for all time. But that is not all. Spiritual cookies play a big part. So even if, in conversation you mention someone else, they too are drawn into the web which means that you have a network fingerprint, or netprint which not only identifies you but everyone you have ever been in contact with.

So for those who say they want someone out of their life, it is an impossibility. And the spirits have been and will always be dealing with this factor. Sometimes it is invaluable and would be used extensively by physical forces if they only knew, but it equally has the opposite and disastrous effect.

Chapter 4

The atmosphere in the house was again electric. Maria was home and starting to prepare the dinner. She'd checked to see that the arsehole wasn't anywhere and assumed he must be at work but she certainly wasn't going to ring to find out. If he was coming back it would be about six thirty but she wouldn't see much of him as she was going to Mum's. She'd offered to pick Joan up on the way so was on a time limit and decided to leave his dinner on a plate if he wasn't home by the time she went and he could stick it in the microwave, if he was capable of doing it, if not he could go without for all she cared. He was lucky to have a meal at all.

A knock at the door made her jump. Couldn't be him, he had a key.

She peeped through the front window and saw Bill at the door.

"Hello Bill." She greeted him.

"You alright duck?" He stood still, making no move to come in.

"Oh yes thank you, and also thank you for last night, I'm afraid I wasn't very communicative."

"Oh don't bother about that. How is he?" His head inclined inside.

"Don't know. He's not here. Look I'd ask you in only I've got to get round my mum's."

"No, No, I didn't want to come in, just wanted to know you were alright. We all wondered about you."

"You're very kind Bill and thank you again."

"Anything, anytime, you just call if you need us."

With a little wave he turned and went back towards his own house but Maria could help noticing that his wife and a couple of her cronies were waiting for him.

"Hmm, sent him to find out." She thought as she went back into the kitchen. "Bet they all sit round the cauldron at night."

Just before half past six she heard the familiar sound of the key in the door. She didn't speak, just let him walk in and eyed him up and down.

"Fit enough for work then?" She finally uttered quite sarcastically.

"Much better thanks." He looked at her very unsure as to what was coming next.

"I'm starting mine because I'm going to mum's with Aunt Joan."

"Why, what's happened?" He stopped on his way out of the kitchen.

"Well, nothing I hope. But we are going together sometimes. It's not easy, not that you care. If you can't shag it, it's not important."

He knew better than to add any comment and went off for a wash.

By the time he came back down, she'd finished and washed everything bar his plate which was on the table ready for him. She didn't ask how he was, or how his cock was, and as long as he kept it well away from her, that was fine.

Before long she was on her way, turned into Joan's road and pulled up at her house. Her aunt was ready and waiting and locked the door before hurrying down to the car.

"You don't have to gallop," Maria laughed "I can wait a minute you know."

"Don't like to keep folks waiting when they are good enough to give me a lift." Joan always thought of others. "Wonder what we'll find tonight."

"You do don't you, wonder I mean."

"Well," Joan seemed eager to impart her snippet, "this Frank, the one I was telling you about has been very helpful."

"Frank?" Maria was concentrating on her driving.

"The lad who does mental work, and he helps with the elderly to do with the shop."

"Right."

"Well, he says of course he can't just barge in, it has to go through the right channels. But he's told me how to go about it and if someone comes round we'll say it's just a friend."

"Just like that?" Maria wasn't listening fully.

"Well the doctor puts her through a test of sorts first then recommends her to the mental health lot."

"But she won't go. Not if we tell her that's what it's for."

Joan sighed.

"But we don't, we just say it's her annual check up. All older people have to have them. I do."

"Do you?"

There was a slight pause before Joan answered.

"Well no, but she won't know that."

They drove in silence for the rest of the short journey but just as they were getting out Joan said quite casually. "You'll really like Frank."

It didn't occur to Maria till later what she'd said. Why would she like Frank? She may never meet him, it could be a totally different person that came, if anyone did, it may not get that far. Something made a little light pop on in her brain.

"What's the canny beggar up to I wonder."

Frank was, as he put it in his late thirties, but to be precise he was only a few months off his fortieth birthday. He was the sort everyone liked but really knew very little about. His co-workers had tried to introduce him to various females but he always declined the offers so then the query came up that he must be gay and yet didn't seem to be attracted to men. As some people must fit everyone into a specific box it was decided he was asexual so they tended to give up on any match making.

In fact he was a very loving person, and would have been more than pleased to meet the right lady, but despite a few relationships, he never felt it was right and so it never worked out for him. Although age was never really a factor, there was a certain stopping point at which he shut off. There had been occasions where married women had thrown themselves at him for a bit of excitement but that was taboo and he didn't go there. He wasn't bad looking and it seemed such a shame he couldn't settle down with someone who could make him happy.

As he made himself comfy on the sofa for the evening he reached for the tv remote then stopped. Joan's conversation was in his mind and for some reason he wanted to know more.

"Hang on." He thought. "Why are you taking such an interest? It's just the same as the countless cases you see every day."

But sometimes we feel our path is laid before us and we must follow it. He knew he had to help Joan in whatever way he could but of course stick to protocol. As he switched on the set he knew his life was about to change but little guessed what was in store.

Dick was not only relieved that his wife would be out of the way for a while but already aroused by the call he would make as soon as the coast was clear. And if all went to plan this would be a freebie.

A new customer had come to pick up her car that afternoon and after she'd settled the paperwork and was about to drive out, Dick had leaned slightly into the open window and given her one of his innocent chat up lines.

"I'd get your old man to keep an eye on that spare wheel, just to be safe."

"Oh thank you," she'd smiled looking straight at him "but that won't be necessary."

"I wouldn't want anything to happen to you. Must be careful."

"I always am. And I don't have an 'old man' as you put it."

Here was an opening and even a come on.

"Well a young one then." He laughed.

"Oh you mean my chauffeur?" Then seeing the shocked look on his face added "Only kidding, not in that class."

"No, but you could be." He wasn't letting this go until he knew he was onto a certainty.

She reached in the glove compartment for a pen, pulled his hand into the car and wrote a phone number on his wrist.

With that she drove off leaving him gobsmacked to say the least. He would never have admitted it wasn't his charm that had worked and he never gave it a thought that this could be another in Cyn's profession.

To him she was quite tasty and what she'd got she didn't keep hidden. Decent knockers, and thighs that went right up to heaven if he was lucky. She seemed a bit younger than his normal pickings, but hey, if she was willing he'd need his brains examining to refuse. And she must have fancied him mustn't she? He was well aware he was physically out of action for a few days but that wouldn't stop him doing the groundwork for now and he could explain, well lie about being busy until he was capable again. Shouldn't sound too available anyway, made you look desperate.

He'd wait until Maria had been gone for a few minutes before calling because you never knew if she would come back just to catch him out.

His demon spirits were on form. This had been no chance encounter for they had so many sexual partners lined up for him he would feel like a kid in a sweetshop, until he was sick. The good angels were fighting them all the way but this cell seemed more powerful than usual and not one Sofia had encountered before but that didn't mean anything.

The whole earth area was rife. For every good power there was always an opposing one but the main threat was when several congregated in one place thinking there was an abundance of likely souls to snatch. But that could be worked to advantage for when evil fights evil the attention is drawn to their contesters in order to beat them and take the spoils, and can be directed away from the good forces. It all comes down to elements assuming they are in charge and letting their defences slip. That's when the good seizes its chance and therefore must be ever watchful even if the odds appear to be against them at that moment. The secret is knowing just when to strike.

"Hi Mum, it's us."

Maria opened the door and made her way to the front room.

"Oh you've come have you?" Was the greeting without Beaty turning to speak.

"Why, what's the matter?"

Silence apart from a huff.

"Hello Beaty." Joan went and stood in front of her.

Looking from one to the other her sister said "Oh that's how it is. I see nobody for weeks then they all come at once."

Maria sighed but before she could speak her aunt cut in.

"Can't you remember? We take it in turns and come every night to make sure you're clean and have a meal."

"I've seen no one." Was the curt reply.

"Mum," Maria started but was cut off.

"Oh you've turned up as well have you? Well I've had to manage haven't I. Nobody cares any more. I could be dead."

This was too much for Maria and she turned and ran into the kitchen sobbing her heart out.

"Well I hope you're satisfied." Joan was in no mood for ingratitude. "That girl goes to work to earn a living, goes home, cooks a meal for her and Dick then comes here every other night to see to you. I come here on the other nights. Now tell me how that isn't caring."

Beaty turned away.

"Oh well if it's too much trouble. I don't want to be a burden to anybody. Everyone's got their own lives to lead."

"Now just a minute. What about when gran was getting on, you used to do the same, and very well may I say."

"Oh yes I used to go down didn't I and you used to come when you could, and we used to do her washing."

Joan sat down.

"That's right Beaty, you see you can remember everything from when we were young, even going to school."

"I can. And do you remember that song we used to sing about the river?"

Without prompting she sat in her chair and sang the whole song word perfect.

Joan's eyes were glistening as she said softly "But you can't remember what's happened recently and that's not your fault."

Beaty looked at her not quite understanding if this was right.

"Can't I? I thought I had a good memory."

"It happens to many of us when we get older. Maria says it's as though our brains are computers. What we did years ago has been saved on the hard drive, but what we do now we don't save it, so it gets deleted."

It was obvious this was all a bit too complicated for her so Joan stood up and said "I'll make you a nice cup of tea then bring your dinner in."

She left her sitting there and went to join her niece in the kitchen. The two hugged for a moment, no words needed but they knew this was going to be a rough ride. It always is when it's one of yours because they aren't the same people you have known before.

"You'll have to get your arse over here pronto tonight." Cyn was buzzing.

Amy held the phone away from her and looked at it.

"Oh yes, and what makes you think I will?"

"Because we are onto some bigger stuff."

"Well I'm working as you know."

Amy was trying to sound offhand but the cash would be very handy as she had a red overdue bill sitting looking at her.

"You finish at ten." Cyn was insistent and hadn't noticed the change in tone and carried on. "But not here. We've got to go to some bloke's place were there will be a few eager knobs waiting."

"And you'll take your pick and I'll be left with the horrible ones." Amy was in a petulant mood.

"It's not like that. This is different. Anyway you can have first grab. OK?"

"What? I mean, I'm not sure." Amy wasn't feeling very comfortable with this but the pound signs rose to the fore again.

"You'll be fine. And I'll explain on the way. Get round here as soon as you get home."

"But I'll have to change." Amy was still uncomfortable as her guardians were trying to prevent her from going by niggling at her mind with all sorts of doubts.

"Don't bother, got it all here."

Cyn's reply was more of an order and when Amy had pressed the off button she said "Yes ma'am".

When the coast was clear Dick dialled the number. He'd wiped it off his wrist before he got home but put it in his phone along with many others.

"Hello." It didn't sound like the same woman and he realised he hadn't even taken her name.

"Um, I'm not sure if I've got the right number, sorry."

"Oh I think you have."

"Right, um did you by any chance take your car into the garage today."

"Oh, no you want my daughter unless I can be of any assistance." He wasn't so blasé now.

"Oh bloody hell what have I got into?" He cursed under his breath but said "I don't want to disturb her if she's busy."

"I'm not busy." The voice was different so they had obviously passed the phone between them.

"Oh you had me worried there for a minute." He gave a nervous laugh.

"I knew you'd call." The voice purred into his ear. "You have a lovely body."

"Oh, well, yes, I mean so do you." He was getting aroused.

"When can we meet?"

"Well, um, I slipped and have hurt my back and have to rest it for a couple of days." Was all he could come up with and as soon as the words had left his mouth he regretted it.

"Really. You didn't seem too bad when I saw you."

"Well I had to go in late, you can ask any of the lads and I was on light work today."

"So when will your – er- back be better do you think."

"Oh its improving already, should be fine in a day or two."

"By the weekend?"

Panic set in. He was ok for a night but if she was going to want him to go away, he'd have to find a brilliant excuse to give to Maria who wouldn't believe him anyway and who knows what she would do when he got back.

"Just what did you have in mind?" He asked as casually as he could.

"Well Mum's got this friend with a cottage in the country and we are going down but I'm going to feel a bit out of it if you get me."

"Oh your mum's going too."

She laughed. "Don't worry, there are two bedrooms and they aren't together, besides there's some lovely walks in the woods. The outdoors really makes me sexy. Do you?"

"Do I what?"

"Feel sexy when you are at one with nature."

This wasn't quite what he expected.

"I can't say I've ever, I mean that isn't to say I wouldn't give it a go."

"Oh there's nothing like it. You'll be hooked."

Maria still came into his mind but he just had to try this and hopefully his ailment should be fine by then.

"Nothing ventured," He started to say.

"Good, that's settled then. Where shall I pick you up?"

"Oh Christ not from home!" Was his first panic reaction. "How about that little park near the garage?"

"Wonderful. About ten?"

"Yes, that would be.... I'll be there. Um when do we come back?"

She laughed. "You aren't even there yet. Sunday evening silly."

"Oh, right. I'll um, yes good stuff."

"One more thing," she purred "you won't need many clothes."

The call had ended and he sat there wondering what had happened. He hadn't felt in charge throughout the whole conversation, she had made all the arrangements. He had feared at first that her mother was going to come on to him and that thought made him cringe. But now all he had to do was find a suitable excuse to be away all weekend.

Sofia was communicating with her superiors concerning the amount of earth time Beaty had left. In cases like this it wasn't the usual thing to cut someone's life short just because they had an illness, albeit physical or mental because it was obvious they would never improve. She was well aware that her charge had to let her span run its course, but was keen to make the running as smooth as they could and cause as little distress to her family as possible. She had a few years yet before she could be released into total spirit and when she was asleep and working with Sofia she was aware off this. Each time she wished she didn't have to go back to body but knew from experience it had to be.

The spirits had many tasks in all areas so it meant that Beaty couldn't always keep an eye on Maria while she was occupied elsewhere, but whenever she could she tried to visit and give her as much protection as possible. It saddened her to see the effect she was already having on her daughter and sister but knew there was nothing in her power that she could do about it. Such is the difference between states of existence.

Sofia had been watching the trio and decided that some time should be allocated for them to meet solely on the spiritual level. So that night she would arrange for Beaty to be in presence when they both slept. Firstly Maria would be guided to sleep followed by Joan then for a short time they could all converse on the same level but it would not be on a regular basis, in fact it may be that this would be their only chance, so they had to make the most of it.

Few people realise that when they say "I just nodded off" that the slumber was induced for a reason. Sometimes spirits will try to get a message into your head but if you aren't receptive they have to resort to stronger means. So they put you to sleep, and when you wake up you wonder where you've been. But it was essential at that time to get certain facts to your spirit.

Amy always got nervous when she didn't know what was going on and she felt that Cyn was going to spring something on her that she didn't feel comfy with. She'd still gone dressed for action, more to give herself confidence than anything.

"Right, let's get going." Cyn said before the other woman was even through the door.

"Umm, where is it like, I mean where we off to?"

"Don't you bother your brain about that," she'd like to have added "not that you'd understand." but kept her mouth shut.

"I'd better have another wee." Amy started to go towards the toilet.

"No time for that. Anyway why didn't you go before you came out?"

"I did, but I'm nervous." And ignoring her friend she disappeared into the lav.

Cyn was tapping her keys on a little shelf when she came back, snorted and indicated for her go so she could lock the door. Amy noticed she had a small suitcase with her.

"Is that what we gotta put on?"

"Just get in the frigging car." Was almost screamed but in an undertone. The neighbours were nosey enough as it was without announcing everything.

In a short time they were on the other side of town heading out into the country. A few times Amy almost started to ask where they were going but thought better of it. Without indicating, they turned off the road and were heading along a small lane towards a building.

"Didn't know this was here." Amy said without thinking.

"Very few do. That's the idea."

"But what if people couldn't find it?"

Cyn didn't come out with the remark she would loved to have used but instead said quietly "We did."

"But...."

The look told Amy not to go on with it. End of.

Although the place was not very obvious from the lane, Cyn still drove round to the back of the building and pulled up near what looked like a delivery door.

"Here we are." She got out and reached into the back of the car for the bag then started towards the small entrance without even checking that Amy was following her.

"Who lives here?"

Cyn faced her. "Look, there's one thing we don't do. We don't ask bloody stupid questions. We don't ask people what they do for a living, they can say, but do not ask. About anything. We're here to do a service for which we will get paid then go home. Is that clear enough for you?"

"Well alright. But there's no need to be......."

"Good. Just remember it if you want to work with me."

It wasn't just two working women that entered when the door was opened. The surround area was full of mischievous demons all here for the entertainment, especially if they could manipulate it. There was also an evil cell looking for another foothold and with some of the clients, this would be a choice base from which to operate. Although slightly outnumbered the good angels were always with their individual subjects which wasn't just the two workers, but the visitors. Had they all been in body, the place would have been bulging and probably very entertaining for any onlooker. But of course the spiritual level is just as attractive for observation.

The visit to Beaty hadn't flowed all that easily and the ladies voiced their thoughts as they went home.

"It's never going to get better is it?" Joan was first to speak.

"It's like it's not her any more." Maria was feeling quite emotional. "Do you think it will speed up?"

"You can't tell. Everyone isn't the same." Joan paused then said "We've had some come into the shop for ages and they've gradually got more forgetful, but there's others that suddenly don't come and when you ask they say that they aren't capable of coming out on their own."

"As quick as that?" Maria was afraid her mum may go the same way.

"Can be but like I say, we're all different. You can't make a general rule."

"So Mum could go on for a bit?"

Joan took a deep breath.

"Haven't you noticed how bad her short term memory is already? Now how long has that been happening without our noticing?"

They had reached Joan's house and she asked Maria if she wanted to come in and settle before she went home.

"Ok. Just for a minute." She didn't move to get out of the car. "I feel so guilty."

"You mustn't. Oh people do but it's not their fault, it's not our fault."

"But I feel it is."

Joan opened the door.

"Inside. This isn't the place to discuss this."

And she got out knowing that her niece would have to follow.

Once they were in the privacy of the lounge, Joan asked if she'd like a drink.

"I ought to get back, but do you know, I don't want do."

"I think we'll have a cuppa anyway. Can't offer you anything stronger with you driving."

A few minutes later the two were sitting on the sofa cup in hand.

"Right lady. Now you can tell me what's gone on. I only got the gist of it when I was in the shop and didn't want to go into it while we were dealing with Beaty so......"

Maria put her cup on the table.

"Quite simple. He came home in agony. Whatever slag he'd been with had obviously bitten his cock, whether for pleasure or revenge or disappointment, I've no idea."

"And......" Joan knew there had to be more.

"That's about it."

"So what did you do, pat him on the head and say good boy? Come on girl, I know you better than that."

"Well, I suppose it needed attention and I suppose I did give him some first aid on it."

"First aid? I've have brought the old family bible down on it I can tell you."

Maria gave a shortened version of her treatment but when she got to the anaesthetic bit Joan gave a hoot.

"I knew it. Well, I should think you did. He's lucky that's all he got. Some would have chopped it off."

For the first time Maria smiled.

"That's funny because one of the neighbours asked that when he came home. You know asked if it had been chopped off."

"Well it's not for me to say, but he deserves all he gets. And you don't like me telling you but he's no good for you and the sooner you can get shut of him the better."

They both sat pondering for a moment then Maria said "That's the trouble, I've had my mind on him when it should have been on Mum."

Joan swung round to face her.

"Now just you listen to me my girl. You've got two things on you mind to worry about. Yes of course we both worry about your mum, my sister, of course we do, but you live with him. You're under the same roof. How can that not affect you all the time?" She paused before adding "Wondering what he's with."

They both sat mulling that one over when Joan suddenly jumped and asked "You're not letting him have his way with you as well are you?"

"Aunt Joan. No, we're not having sex. I couldn't stand him touching me."

"Well I'm very glad to hear it because, well you know, diseases and things."

"Yes, I'd thought of that." Maria assured her.

"But how can you live with him?"

"Because, I don't think I could keep that place on with just my wages."

"You need his money." Joan was thinking aloud. "Got it. You come and live with me."

"Oh I couldn't, I mean..." This had never occurred to Maria and it was a kind suggestion, but she didn't really want to live in someone else's house. She's made this one her own and didn't really want to leave it, but she'd be happy if he went if it wasn't for the running costs.

"Well, we don't need to do anything now, but just keep it on the back burner. You'll always be more than welcome here you know that."

They both hugged for a moment then Maria decided she had better go, not that she was looking forward to it but it had to be like this for now.

As she drove back, the same thing happened. She realised the car was slowing down, but in fact it wasn't mechanical, she just didn't want to go to where he was. She couldn't take it much longer but should she leave him or get him to leave her?

As soon as Joan had been left alone her mind turned to Frank. Now there was a nice young man. If Maria could meet him and like him, maybe she would realise there was more to life than being stuck with a dick! It would be tricky as he made it plain he had nothing to do with married ladies, but a friendship wouldn't hurt, that could be made quite plain right from the start. So while Beaty was being helped with her illness , so could these two, but they just had to meet. Well she'd soon see to that. Her mind was made up and when she set her heart to something she didn't give up. The main thing was not to appear obvious so this would call for underhand methods. She'd used many in the past with stunning results. After all, few knew it but she would never have married the one of her choice if it had been left up to him. Frank wouldn't even know he was being manipulated and if his feelings started to drift in a certain direction, she'd make sure he wasn't going to ignore them. Of course Maria would know nothing of her involvement apart from Beaty's care, and it's always nice to have someone to lean on. She gave a quick thought to their ages. Ten years. Well that was nothing. And so the mental hook had been cast, now to reel them in.

"Cup of tea, I've just made one."

For one split second Maria thought she must be in the wrong house. Her husband offering her a drink? Her instincts told her he'd either just been up to something or was about to embark on another conquest.

"Oh just get on with it and leave me alone," was her thought as she went into the kitchen. Barely looking at him she said "I'm ok thanks."

He followed her into the lounge and the air was so full of false sweetness it was like waiting for a storm to break. She flopped into the nearest chair.

"So what is it this time?" She said with the most uninterested tone she could muster.

"How do you mean? And how was your mum?" He tried to change the subject.

"As if you really care. As well as can be expected but not good."

"Oh, sorry to hear that."

The reply came out almost as though he had selected a button to send a suitable stock answer. She'd noticed he was doing that quite a bit of late almost as though it sounded caring but in fact he was just on automatic.

"Aunt Joan took me back to hers for us both to wind down. It's upsetting seeing Mum like this and it will only get worse."

"Hope all's good her side."

Maria stared at him.

"In what way?"

He looked confused as well he might.

"Eh?"

"Well, it's as bad for her if you think about it."

"Has she got it as well then?"

This was the final straw for Maria, it was like having a conversation with yourself but not so intelligent.

"You've got no feeling for anyone but yourself. You don't care a monkey's bollocks for me, for the family only your floosies. But if things don't go right for you, oh dear. Everybody must know about it."

"What the hell you bleating on about now?" He stood and blocked her way. "Did I broadcast what happened to me? No I did not. Did I run round naked showing all the nosey old buggers who were baying for blood? No I did not. Did I........."

"Oh shut up you're delirious. She must have infected you with something so don't you lay a finger on me, don't even come near me."

As she went towards the door he grabbed her arm and yelled in her face.

"Do you know I was going to sit down and discuss something with you, all nice like, and we would have had a decent discussion but no, you don't want that. You want to knock me down then trample all over me. Talk about bollocks? I'm surprised you haven't cut mine off while I was asleep."

With that he threw her against the wall. Her temper was rising.

"Why the hell don't you just piss off out of my life before I do something I'll regret, no something you'll regret for the rest of your miserable existence.

"May I remind you that I pay the mortgage on this place." His face was inches from hers.

"And I pay most of the frigging bills in case you'd forgotten."

He pulled back a pace or two and stood staring at her. She wasn't sure whether to move in case he went for her so she returned his stare.

With a deep sigh he put his head to one side so condescendingly and said "You see, what you don't understand about me is that I tell other women that you are such a major part of my life that they have to live with it and if they can't it's their problem."

Her mouth dropped open.

"In case you had forgotten. I am your wife."

There was silence as she waited for his reply but he just looked at her as if that was the end of it.

"In case you don't get what that means," she said very precisely "it means they should not be a tiny part of your life. Do you get that?"

His next comment nearly made her explode.

"I refer to the reply I have just given you." He stared ahead is if she wasn't even in the room.

"What?" Her eyes were ablaze and she was shaking with fury. "Are you mad?"

Again. "I refer to the reply I have just given you."

He knew very well what he was doing. In the past when she had faced him with some of his actions and he didn't want to lie, he would give silly answers but now he had found this new weapon. Keep giving a politician's reply and drive her crazy while he stayed perfectly calm. And it worked.

As she went to punch him in the mouth, he ducked, grabbed her wrist and hissed into her face "Don't even think about it bitch!" Then he swung her round until she stumbled and hit the floor. With a smirk he left the room.

The adjoining elderly neighbours couldn't miss the commotion and turned the telly down so they could hear more, their ears pressed to the wall.

"Is he hitting her?" The wife asked.

"Don't know, but he's giving her what for. Can't make it all out but something about his bollocks."

"You don't have to repeat it like that. It's not polite." His wife tried to appear disgusted but then said "What else?"

"Sshh. I think she said she's got a knife."

"I'd have used it on him a long time ago."

Her husband waved his arm to tell her to be quiet.

"I can't hear if you're talking."

"Well you're talking." she thought to herself.

"I think something's been thrown at the wall. Now she's yelling but I can't hear him."

They both stood for a moment then she whispered "It's all gone quiet."

They looked at each other for a moment before he said "D'you reckon she's done him one."

His wife's hand shot to her mouth. "Oh heaven preserve us."

As there seemed to be no sign of any more activity, the husband said "I think I'll just have a word with Bill, he knows 'em better than us."

"I'll come too." She wasn't going to be left out of this.

Together they went out into the little garden at the front of the house and were greeted by a few more of the neighbours who hurried up to them asking what they knew. It seems the argument had travelled further than they thought.

"You must know, you are attached to them." One said.

"But we couldn't hear much except shouting." The husband said not wanting to say anything that he wasn't one hundred percent sure of. Unfortunately his wife was the opposite and liked to be first with any fresh bit of news.

"Well we did think she said she had a knife."

That sent a buzz round the crowd which was growing by the minute. If anything happened in the small crescent, everyone soon heard about it. Bill tried to calm things down by saying they didn't know for certain and not to jump to conclusions but some had other ideas.

"He could be lying there dead now."

"But what if he got the knife off her?"

"They could both have had a knife."

"Seems a bit too quiet to me."

Bill had heard enough.

"Alright. Alright. I'll go and see."

That brought a ripple of agreement and they couldn't wait for him to come back with the gossip.

"P'raps she's cut his dick off." One comment started a new chuckle.

"Why does his dick always have to come into it?" A woman said.

"Well it's been in most other places." Was the retort.

They would have elaborated but the door had been opened and Bill was talking to Dick. Everyone strained to listen but everything was said so quietly, but they knew Bill would tell them everything in a minute. So the comments continued.

"Well she hasn't cut his dick off."

"Will you shut up about it. We hear nothing else."

"She hasn't done him in."

"So where is she then?"

"Hang on. What's happening."

Bill had taken a few steps back and was looking up at the bedroom window. Everyone could hear Dick yelling up the stairs.

"Will you put your head out of the window and prove I haven't topped you? They all think I've have."

The answer was clear to Bill and almost audible to the others.

"Good. Let them think that. You might as well have."

Then complete silence.

Bill said goodnight and as the door shut, he turned and joined the rest of the neighbours.

"Well?"

"It's OK, they had a bit of a row that's all. Got a bit hot under the collar but its all over so we can all go back indoors."

There were a few disappointed mutters but there was nothing else for it so everyone returned to their own place, until the next time of course.

Chapter 5

Sofia had to wait until Joan and Maria were asleep before she could bring the ladies together. She had already planned with their angels how they would organise it as it could be every emotional for the two still in body and no one is ever sure how these things will go. As ever, they also had to be aware of the evil presences for at such times it could leave the souls of the participators open to attack.

Whenever anyone is down, or not protecting their guard, the evil elements jump at the opportunity to take them over and really play with their emotions often resulting in long term or even permanent damage. Also people are subject to suggestion which is why it is often said "I'd never have thought it of him/her in a million years" because somebody has done something completely out of character, but absolutely anyone can be groomed, even to commit murder. Also if anyone thinks badly of another, they will take control making that person's feelings exaggerated so that they feel malice which they think comes from them, but they are only the host. So the kindest hearted person could be used to spread evil.

Beaty was already waiting with Sofia as they hovered over their family.

"Do you know the worst thing about this disease?" She asked her angel.

"Being an observer."

Beaty had to think for a moment then she knew what Sofia was getting at.

"Yes. That's right. You watch the world going on around you but you aren't part of it."

Sofia said "Well we accept that it can vary in different people but I think from observation it doesn't help when people speak over them, not to them. They feel they aren't there."

"Yes that's right. I was with a lady who seemed to be right out of it and everyone was looking for a certain form they needed and she turned to the helper and pointed to a green folder and said 'It's in there.' So the helper told the family who said they'd already looked. Well, she suggested they look again, and lo and behold there it was."

"Exactly. They aren't treated as having any sense or knowledge."

"Suppose I'll have to go through that." Beaty didn't relish the thought.

"But you do have an advantage." Sofia reminded her. "When you sleep you can resume your duties and have a break from it."

"Hmm. Pity you can't remember when you wake up."

Sofia was alert. Joan was now asleep so they'd give her a few seconds to settle then take her with them.

"Hello." It seemed a strange greeting as one would expect her to be shocked but in a dream we never question who is there or why and she would later think she had dreamt, if they allowed her to remember.

Joan's angel let Sofia do all the explaining and it did seem to take a bit of understanding at first. But they had to be ready for when Maria went to sleep to have their conference.

"So I won't know any of this?" Joan asked.

Her angel answered now "Maybe some when you first wake but as the day goes on you forget." She let that sink in then added "You know when you have that sort of dream that stays with you all day and seems to be very real?"

"Oh yes. I've had those." Joan agreed. She wasn't even surprised now that she was communicating with angels.

"Well, that's when you've had an encounter, like you are now."

For the first time Joan realised that Beaty looked the same as these other two.

"Oh god. You've died."

They all saw the humorous side and Sofia explained.

"No, your sister has the ability to be aware of her spiritual side but only when she is asleep, and she is a good worker."

"Worker? Don't we ever get away from it?"

If all else failed they knew this was going to be a very entertaining session.

A message coming in from Maria's guardian alerted them and in a split second they were above her bed waiting for her to be deep enough to take her.

They all moved well away from the area while Sofia explained the purpose of this meeting.

"When there are several factors which will test the person to their limits, it is advisable to give them a bolt hole which is why some people appear to cope better than others. You Maria have the worry of your Mum in body, but here you can relax and see her as her true self. She can also be relieved that you are not just coping with her physical side which is distressing you. Although you won't remember in your waking hours, this break will give you the inner strength to cope. But you also have another burden. Your husband. Now how you cope with that in body is up to you, but when you are taken out of the picture, you may think more clearly and make the right decisions. And we are all here to help, we are a team."

Maria was overcome that the ones closest to her would still be by her side so she wasn't alone. Already she was feeling strength and relief she couldn't explain.

Then Sofia turned to Joan.

"You think you are here to support Maria and because of your care for your sister when she is awake in body."

Joan agreed, but then Sofia continued.

"You will also meet Beaty when you both sleep and regain your strength but there is more in your case."

Both Maria and Joan were wondering what was going on.

"Is Aunt going to have dementia too?" It was a question laden with sadness.

"No, No. Nothing like that."

There was almost an audible sigh of relieve from the three ladies.

Sofia let the thought settle then added "There is going to be something in your life which will test you to the limits. That is why in this group you too can draw strength to help you make the right decisions because it will be in your hands."

"But what is it?" She wanted to know but Sofia indicated that was all for now. The only thing she would tell her was that when the time came she would know.

After Cyn had given a certain knock on the door it was opened a fraction and when the man saw who it was he opened the door quickly and ushered them in.

"You've got this. Wait until you're called."

He indicated a small room which turned out to be a small cloakroom with a toilet.

"Many?" Cyn asked without looking at him.

"Enough." Was all she got in reply.

When he'd gone Amy, who was feeling very uneasy, watched as Cyn unpacked the small bag. What had her friend got her into?

"Right that's yours. Hope you've only got a thong."

Amy looked at the leather outfit, if you could call it that and was horrified to see that it didn't cover very much.

"I've never worn anything like this." She picked it up as though it was dirty. "Is it new?"

"Well, almost." Cyn was already undressed.

"What do you mean, almost?" Amy was ready to leave.

"Well I tried it on once, that's all. You don't think I'd give you something I haven't checked out do you? Not in this business."

For a moment there was silence then Amy asked "Have you had many other people working with you?"

"A few, why?"

"And did they, I mean, wear this kind of gear?"

"Depends on what was called for. Like tonight."

Cyn knew this wasn't going to be easy but she hadn't got anyone else to bring with her. She'd lied about having others as she didn't get on with many of her kind and had always worked alone, but if a job called for two women, she had to find someone or lose out, so she collared one that wouldn't have a clue, until she trained her, and she could rake in the fee.

"Look love, let me just put you straight. This is different, you don't give them sex, OK?"

"What?"

"Just listen up, we haven't got long. These are business folk, blokes in charge, in authority and they have to unwind by not being top dog for a while. Get it?"

"Ummm."

"They won't be in charge tonight, we will be. They have to do what we tell them or they will get punished. Here have a quick gander at this."

She pulled a small pamphlet out of her bag and thrust it into Amy's hand. She hadn't dare tell her before as she knew she wouldn't have come. Well she got that bit right.

"This is awful, they're ugly and look how old that one is. And she's got a whip."

At which point Cyn pulled her own out of the bag.

"You mean we smack them?"

"Yes, smack, kick, spit in their face, look whatever they want we do but no sex. Now have you got this? It's money, that's why we're here and," she paused "I want to be called again so don't make a balls of it."

"Are they posh?" Amy still wasn't happy.

"If they were that posh we wouldn't be here."

The man tapped on the door but came in anyway.

"Ready?"

"As much as we'll ever be." Cyn muttered. As they followed him she whispered to Amy, "Just stick with me for a start and don't look as though you're new to this."

They were ushered into a room with about six men in it.

"Is this it?" Cyn whispered.

The man shrugged. "More were booked but cancelled. This should be enough for you."

"Ok gentlemen," Cyn eyed them up. "What we're doing tonight as you are a very select group, is...." she looked round them all slowly "we are going to see you one by one and decide which of us you prefer."

One or two looked a bit surprised but the others nodded in agreement. What the girls didn't know was that this was the first time for most of them so they didn't quite know what to expect.

There were two rooms that had been allocated in this old house where the gentlemen could have their pleasure. The place had been empty for some time and really they had no right to be there which was why it was always very hush hush, but the couple that ran the proceedings also thought they could make a fast buck this way so the women were in their own league. This was the very bottom of the scale, so the men were only paying accordingly.

"Right, who'd like to be first?" Cyn cracked her whip which startled some of them. "Nobody brave enough? Well …" she turned to Amy "You choose."

Amy nearly choked but looked at the most nervous and said quickly "Him."

"If you'd like to come with us sir." She held out her arm to him but spoke to the rest. "Won't be a moment, don't be impatient, you'll all get your turn."

There was never a more amateur exit from a room than the three disappearing through the door.

Once in the room Cyn went straight to work.

"And what have you been doing you naughty boy?"

The poor chap looked from one to another.

"Um well, I….."

"Get down on the floor you dog." Cyn yelled so loud that Amy jumped back but Cyn wasn't letting her get away with anything and the only way to learn was to get down and dirty. As the man got onto he knees she thrust the whip into Amy's hand and said "Punish him. He's been bad."

Amy's face was a picture. She hadn't a clue and as for learning by example, she seemed to have shut her mind to everything.

"Ok got the picture. You can go now and send the next poor sod in." Cyn's voice broke into her reverie.

"Is that it?" She whispered.

"Haven't you heard a thing, now don't cock this up. So that you have some idea what their taste is, we're going through them all to see what they want."

She sighed. What in creation had made her think for one minute this would work? Too late now.

They flew through the preliminaries, and Amy had a vague idea of what was expected and her first actual client was a middle aged man that seemed to be fiddling with his undercarriage all the time.

"Sit over there and be quiet."

He sat down and reached out towards her groin.

"Don't touch." She almost whispered and he had to ask her to repeat it.

The visiting mischievous spirits were having a field day and their mirth attracted more to come and watch this fiasco. Some had veered off for a while to watch Cyn in action but became bored and wanted the fun.

Although the protective angels were doing their best, lust is a great tool and some weren't going to miss any of this.

The man started to undo his trousers.

"What are you doing? You're not supposed to do that. It's bad." Amy thought she had got the hang of this now.

"I need a jerk."

"I'm not here for that." She said quickly.

"Show us your pussy."

"Why?"

He looked at her and stood up, zipped his fly and said "You're a waste of time, I'm not paying for this."

At that moment Cyn appeared in the doorway.

"And just where do you think you're going? Get back on that chair now!"

He was so surprised he sat down heavier than he intended. Cyn indicated Amy to go to the next room and start on the next specimen while she gave this one a run for his money. The tirade of abuse she dealt out could be heard in the corridor. She'd grabbed the whip and the cries were partly of terror but some of enjoyment.

Although the evil lot enjoyed this kind of thing for a while, they had found the incompetence of the other girl much more to their taste and were all in that room waiting for her to make the next blunder.

The angels wanted them both out of there but there was no chance of that so they had no option but to try and protect each one as much as possible.

Amy was beginning to get the gist of what she was expected to do by the time she was servicing the last one and was even riding on his back to the cheers of the invisible onlookers. They were having a ball.

By the time the women had got back into their ordinary clothes all the clients were long gone having been shepherded out in haste. The man walked into the cloakroom, handed Cyn the money and told them to sling their hook this minute. Before they were even in the car, he'd locked the door and was making his way to his vehicle, whatever it was for it was very well hidden.

"That wasn't as bad as I expected." Amy seemed satisfied with herself.

"Don't kid yourself dear. That was about as near the bottom of the pile as you can get but it brings a bit in, no questions asked."

"How much did we get?" Amy was keen to know.

"I'll sort it when we get back."

"You don't know?"

"Got to check it."

Amy turned and looked at her.

"I only get a bit, I know."

"You'll get your share! Of course I have to organise it so obviously I have more, and it was your first time."

Amy grunted hoping this woman wasn't ripping her off and using her.

To change the subject Cyn said as a passing comment "You know we always hope we won't recognise any of them. Can be a bit embarrassing. They always think you could grass on them so makes them wary about coming back."

"Well I didn't know anybody." Amy thought for a minute then asked "You didn't did you?"

"Oh no one that would know me."

"You did. Which one?"

"Not professional to say."

"Oh, I was hoping you were going to tell me."

Most would have said "But you'll tell me anyway." But Amy wasn't 'most'.

"Well, you'll have to promise to keep your mouth shut."

Actually Cyn couldn't wait to say but she liked playing with this imbecile. More savvy people wouldn't have taken her antics and told her where to get off but Amy was leaning on her.

"Of course I will."

"Well, that older chap who kept checking nobody had run off with his pump action, him."

"Yeah?"

"He's Dick's boss."

"Not Maria's Dick?"

"How many Dicks do you know and don't answer that."

"Oo, what if he found out?"

Cyn was pulling into the drive now.

"But that's the point. He won't find out because we aren't going to say anything are we? Code of silence and all that. You promised remember?"

"I promised I won't say anything to Dick."

"Or anybody. Get it into you're your thick skull. You talk, we don't work. Anyway it can lead to other things."

As they went into the house Amy asked "What other things?"

Cyn about threw her stuff on the sofa and faced her friend.

"Do I have to spell everything out for Christ sake?"

"But I didn't know if........"

"Look. Not everyone is a nice person. In our trade we deal with some nasty people." She was being sarcastic but Amy would never notice. "You don't know what connections people have or the lengths they go to in order to cover up their tracks. Now you spill the beans on one, and his friends pop round to see you. OK?"

"What they want some action as well so that's good isn't it?"

"It's not bloody good. You could be found on the floor, in a ditch anywhere. Dead."

That thought brought the conversation to an abrupt halt.

"Um, what about the money?" Amy knew she had to ask.

"Look, I'll sort it in the morning OK?"

There was nothing more Amy could do about it. When Cyn was determined nothing would budge her. As she walked to her own place, an idea crossed Amy's mind. Even the ones that don't appear to be quick on the uptake can be as canny if needs be.

"Well if she doesn't cough up tomorrow, I can always make a phone call." She thought with a smile.

Frank was still thinking about all that Joan had said and for some reason it had stuck in his brain. He came across many people in his work and sometimes one or two might make an impression but usually there were always so many more to deal with. Joan had mentioned her niece several times but as she was married, whether happily or not didn't matter, she was not available but Joan had seemed keen for them to meet. His barrier went up. People had often tried to match make and if he was going to meet the woman of his dreams it would happen and not have to be arranged. His mind turned back to Joan. He really liked everything about her but she must be in her seventies which made her way too old, but perhaps they could be friends. Again he pushed the thought away but it was as though something was insisting he thought about it. He turned over to go to sleep but had a feeling of impending change. Good or bad he didn't know but he would have to keep his shield up in case it could be harmful.

Unbeknown to him Joan's guardian was trying to switch his mind off her because she was certainly sending out waves of attraction in his direction, not for herself but for Maria. Sometimes she had been successful with her mind control but it hadn't been fuelled by good spirits and she felt she had the power to control other's minds especially the quieter ones. There was a certain attachment of evil around her constantly and the angels were aware of this when they had the meeting. Although one can't completely block them because they are as powerful, they can be held away depending on the strength of the good powers. This would be something to consider especially with her closeness to Beaty and Maria. The attachments could easily then hook onto them leaving them vulnerable. Maria's guardian was already adding protection because of Dick so she didn't need any other source muscling in.

Beaty was in her sleep state and very much aware of what had been going on that evening and both she and Sofia knew the impending implication. Maria's guardian had been alerted and was already strengthening the shield around her. But even in the spirit world there are very few secrets except at the much higher levels. So when one power starts up a protection routine, the opposition matches it. To put it simply, as soon as Maria's protective force was applied, the evil side in Dick's domain were alerted and upped their strength. It didn't take them long to work out why for some of them had been doing their own homework and were ready for the balloon to go up.

Joan wasn't ready for her sister's greeting.

"What do you think you are doing?"

Even Sofia was surprised at the sudden outburst.

"Now what are you going on about?" Joan feigned surprise but knew very well Beaty had hooked on to her latest source of attraction.

"Leave Maria alone. She's got enough to cope with as you very well know."

"Which is why a little bit of distraction wouldn't go amiss." Joan seemed quite determined and a little smug.

Sofia quietly entered the conversation.

"Ladies, I know you have always had different ways of dealing with things but the simpler we keep this at the moment, the better. Don't you think?"

"Well I know when I've been put in my place." Joan was definitely peeved.

"Not at all. But we know something is about to erupt and we must keep the vibrations calm."

Her own peace wafted over them, but the demons who were in constant touch with Joan weren't going to let this one go. All three were aware of their presence which was why Sofia liked to give them as little to pick on as possible, as did Beaty but Joan seemed to thrive on the excitement. This was the threat. For she wouldn't be able to stop if things got too nasty and by then it would be too late. They already had her in their power to some extent and that's what they built on. It started with such small control the victim didn't even notice but then they let it grow and eventually run its inevitable course.

They hovered over Maria's bed, waiting. As if on cue the phone rang. She was neither asleep or awake and felt as though she'd had too many drinks, the spirits had seen to that.

"Hello." Her voice was slurred.

"Maria, is that you? You sound weird."

"Oh Amy. What do you want? I'm in bed."

"Lucky you I say."

Maria was now becoming a little irritated. If her friend wanted something for goodness sake why didn't she spit it out.

"What is it Amy?"

"Well.....have I got things to tell you."

"Couldn't it possibly wait until morning, as I say I'm nearly asleep, it's been a hell of a day."

She was still very much in shock after Dick's attack on her and wasn't in the mood for the likes of Amy. She looked over her shoulder. He hadn't come to bed so she might as well let the silly woman say her bit and have done with it.

"Oh no. You wait. Have I got a juicy bit for you?"

Maria pulled herself up a bit and said as sleepily as she could "Go on then, I won't get any peace until you've told me."

"Well, you know that woman I told you about?"

"You'll have to be more specific. What woman?"

This wasn't going to be easy.

Amy was insistent.

"You know. The one, well I don't like to say but the one where someone thought they saw your husband's car that night, well not right outside but it was round the corner, when he came home with his cock nearly bitten off."

This wasn't going well. Maria was tempted to finish the call but she knew the idiot would only ring back so she might as well sit it out. With a big obvious sigh she said "Vaguely."

"Well, she asked me to go out with her tonight and I thought she meant a drink. You know what I mean."

"Oh my god." Maria muttered under her breath wondering if she could stay awake long enough to hear the punch line.

"You'll never guess."

"Never in a million years."

"We went to this place see, and we had to get into these thin leather things and these men were there. Get me?"

"Ahead of you." Maria was nearly nodding from the boredom.

"I'm not joking, the things people want, funny things like, not normal."

"So how many did you have to bully?"

"Eh? You mean you know?" Amy was staggered.

"It's common knowledge you little fool. And you didn't guess?"

"Well I mean I've seen stuff on tv but I didn't think it happened with people you know."

This set off an alarm bell. Maria sat up a bit more and feeling quite alert now.

"Go on. Who did you know?"

Amy giggled childishly.

"Oh we aren't allowed to say, that's part of it, anyway I didn't know him but Cyn did."

"Cyn being your…friend?"

"Course."

Maria hade a gut feeling she was about to find out something she didn't want to know but would have to.

"Well, if you aren't allowed to say, why are you telling me all this?"

"Promise you won't breathe a word 'cause it could get him in trouble and I might not get paid."

"You've not been paid yet? Come on Amy get a grip."

"She didn't want to bother tonight so I'll get it tomorrow."

"I'm not being nosey but has she said how much, just so you know."

"Well no."

Maria knew this woman was using this girl knowing how simple she was and didn't like to see this happen to anyone.

"Now you listen to me. When and if you must lead this sordid life, you always ask first what you will get. You don't know how much she raked in and whether you will get your fair cut."

"But she arranges it."

Maria felt she was fighting a losing battle here and told her to be more savvy with what was going on.

"But I haven't told you who was there." Amy seemed determined to import her juicy bit.

"Thought you said you weren't allowed."

"Well, promise me you won't say anything."

"Look, if you're going to tell me just say it. And I won't tell anyone."

She was past caring now because it couldn't have been Dick, not in his state and he had been too busy knocking her about.

"Right. It was your old man's boss."

"Phil. Oh well that's his business I suppose. It's really got nothing to do with us. Um, how did your friend know him, oh scrub that, obvious I suppose."

"She didn't say, she just knew him that's all. But you mustn't say."

"I wouldn't dream of it." She answered but thought "I went through all that for nothing."

After the usual 'goodnights' the call eventually ended.

The three watchers and the observing audience knew this wasn't going to be the end of this and fate has an unusual way of giving the false impression when let loose.

When Joan woke up she had no recollection of anything including Sofia's warnings, and now the growing evil influence was going to get her on track. They could have some fun with this one and really stir things up for their entertainment. But it went further than that. Once they had her obeying all their instructions they were well on the way to controlling her soul, a fact with which the good forces were only too familiar.

Likewise Beaty woke up wondering what day it was. She knew she should have a wash but wasn't sure if she'd already done it. She got some clean clothes out of the drawer and put them on the bed, then went to the ones she had taken off the night before and put those on instead. As she went downstairs she was sure there was something she had forgotten but couldn't for the life of her remember what it was. Once in the kitchen she knew she should have a drink so turned one of the gas jets on the stove. But then knew she had to fill the electric kettle. She busied about getting a beaker but couldn't remember where the tea was.

"I bet they've moved it again."

She was getting exasperated with whoever called because they put things so she couldn't find them. As she moved near the stove she began to feel the warmth and thought she must have left a gas on so she turned one of the other knobs to put it off but actually turned another one on.

Just when she found the tea bags the phone rang.

"Hello."

"Hello Mum, it's Maria."

"You'll have to speak up. Everyone mutters these days."

"Maria Mum."

"No, not picking you up." And she put the phone down.

It rang again.

"Now who is it this time?" She spoke to herself and nearly didn't answer but then changed her mind.

"Whoever you are speak up."

"Maria Mum. Maria." It was almost shouted.

"Alright, I can hear. You don't have to yell as though I'm deaf."

Maria went almost through a check list to see that everything was alright. When asked if she'd had breakfast Beaty said she thought so.

"Well I'll call in on the way from work, then Aunt Joan is coming in later. OK?"

"There's no need to fuss. I don't want to be a burden on anybody."

"You're not a burden Mum. We come because we love you."

The usual goodbyes were said and as Beaty went back to the kitchen she thought "I'm sure I heard the phone go."

Although Sofia called in extra support during Beaty's waking hours she knew very well it wouldn't have much effect but it did protect her from the likes of those in Joan's vicinity for this was the ideal subject to use to gather more into their ranks. At all costs, Beaty's soul must be under guard until she could pass into total spirit. As is common in this kind of case, it is kinder when they are released from their mortal trappings but while the body can function it will carry on as long as the brain remembers to give it nourishment.

Because Cyn's level of performance didn't attract the high spenders and only got her in with the lower end of the scale, she had to accept the kind of tactics such organisers used without question. So when the number of expected participants dropped, so did what she got paid. The man's attitude was that if he didn't rake it in, nor did she. The promises of £300 per client were non existent and as only six had turned up she hadn't serviced as many so didn't have to work so hard. She didn't know what they paid although she had tried to find out from them. He didn't have to pay for the premises because that was done without anyone's knowledge except bribing one who had kept a key and also wanted to make a fast buck.

So when he'd slipped Cyn her money and hurried them out she didn't actually check it, like most would, until she got home. She hit the roof and was on the phone to him straight away.

"Two hundred quid!" She exploded. "That's not what we agreed."

"Look lady, we didn't get the full shot. And you brought a bloody junior that you had to train. She don't count."

"Now look matey, we still entertained six blokes who were all bleeding pleased with what they got. You've welshed."

"And what are you going to do about it? If you can't stand the pace, don't play with the big boys."

"Big boys! Get your brain fixed buster. You ain't the big league."

"You never will be you skanky whore. Just take what's on offer, while it is on offer." The rest of his descriptive profanities can only be imagined.

"You haven't heard the last of this. I'll blast your filthy ways round the business, then we'll see."

If he was going to come back with any further suitable suggestions she didn't hear them as the phone was clicked off and thrown across the room.

She was woken by the phone ringing.

"Cyn? It's me."

She knew Amy would be after her money but in the middle of the night?

"I'll sort it in the morning now piss off."

"It is morning. I'm at my cleaning job. When are you going to pay me? I need it."

"Christ almighty! You need it, I need it. We all frigging need it."

"I'll be home at dinner time. You can give it me then."

"Ok Ok, now shut your face and let me get some farting sleep."

The call was at an end and Amy stood there seething. There was no way this bitch was going to get away with it. She was obviously trying to avoid paying and Amy for once wasn't standing for it. It's amazing how when you need money and you know it's owed to you, just how brave you can be demanding your rights.

Lunchtime was going to be very interesting in more ways than one.

Maria was drained and felt ready for her break. She was still shaken from last nights events and although Dick had made an effort at being sociable it hadn't cut any ice with her. It was time for lunch and she decided to go to the local shop and get a sandwich, find somewhere quiet away from people and eat it at leisure. The area offered little privacy and so she wandered away from the office and down a little side street. She'd never been down here before and had no idea where she was going. After a few yards the buildings stopped and she found she was looking down a slope onto what appeared to be a disused railway line. Looking around, she satisfied herself that nobody was about and sat down on the grassy slope which disappeared under a strong fence, obviously constructed to stop anyone tumbling down. She could hear the hum of traffic but this was quite peaceful and she could even hear the odd bird singing.

She had just finished her sandwich when her phone rang disturbing the calmness. It was her husband. Should she answer it? Deciding she'd better but promising herself he wouldn't get to her she pulled it out of her bag and hit the green button.

"Hello." The tone was flat.

"Hi sweetheart."

Her suspicions rose straight away. He only called her endearing names when he either wanted something or had done something.

"What is it?"

She automatically waited for the load of verbal diarrhoea which would undoubtedly follow.

"Well I've been asked to do a favour for a mate."

"Go on."

"See, he, well him and his wife have to go and see her sister at the weekend only he can't drive at the moment and she doesn't so they wondered if I could drive them down like. I'd have to stay over at the cottage and then bring them back Sunday. Won't cost me anything."

"And are you?" She knew the answer before asking it.

"Well what could I say? You help a mate out don't you? I mean he'd do the same for me."

"Oh I'm sure he would." She thought to herself but replied "Well you go. I've got plenty to do what with mum and that."

"You don't mind?" He was obviously saying the right thing even after he'd already said he was going.

"Like I say. You go." Then for some reason she asked "Anyone I know?"

That had been prompted by her guardian to put him on the spot.

"Well actually it's the boss, Phil. Nice chap."

She swallowed hard and after the usual 'Bye' and 'See you later' he'd gone.

She sat for a moment piecing everything together. Glancing at her watch she was alright for a few minutes and she needed to get it right in her brain. Summing it all up she had the fact that Amy had been at a place last night for sexual deviation to give it a handle, Phil had been there as a client, so unless he'd had a lift he had driven himself. Now he needs to go away for the weekend but can't drive.

Her guardian was sending little arrows to her. He's making an excuse. He isn't going with Phil. He's lying. He's got another woman on.

If she could prove any of it she'd get rid of him for good, that way he would have to pay one way or another. She didn't quite know how but one thing was certain she was going to make sure he got his comeuppance for all he was doing to her. She strode back to work with angry determination.

"The filthy bastard." She muttered.

Chapter 6

Sofia needed to communicate with Beaty so sent her into an induced sleep.
"You need to be aware."
This was all that needed to be imparted and Beaty immediately took on board the fact that this was something urgent.
"Can't wait for Joan, we'll fill her in later."
Sofia stayed where she was and they were conversing just above the chair where Beaty was snoring. Quickly she relayed Maria's last call.
"Whether she now wants him or not, this is still going to stress her because she knows he's lying and there's nothing more degrading."
"I wish she would tell me," Beaty was musing "but she will know I'm not understanding anything physically and won't want to confuse me."
"Which brings me to the next point."
"Oh, there's more."
"Well since she's not here, Joan."
"Oh I know she's trying to do her bit of matchmaking."
Sofia agreed but added "It could stress Maria further if your sister starts meddling, although I'm not a hundred percent sure she isn't a bit infatuated herself. Her guardian even thinks she is getting the hook in and then will see which way it goes."
"Oh this is all we need."
They were silent for a second then Sofia said "May need to let you have plenty of naps so we can catch up and nobody will think anything of it. Older people do tend to nod off a lot."
The communication had only taken as long as it takes an eye to blink but both knew they had to be watchful to avoid a disaster.

Beaty opened her eyes, looked round the room, then down at the chair.

"Oh I've done it again."

She laughed totally unaware of what had just gone on in the room. Sofia smiled and rested her hand on the woman's head. The change that took place in seconds was always amazing and it made those in spirit realise the torment some of the people must go through with this illness. Although some may appear happy and blissfully unaware of the real nature of their condition, others experience a never ending living hell. It's a place they don't understand and alien to what has gone on in their life to date. Even their family can seem like strangers that don't understand and start being patronising which is the deepest cut. Their children whom they've nurtured since birth now treat them like imbeciles.

"And how are we today?"

That would grate on them if they still had their mind power and whoever said it, would be told in no uncertain manner.

But sadly this was the path Beaty was following as long as she had breath.

What Sofia hadn't told her was that the evil that had been hovering around Joan had attracted another source even more sadistic than the one in presence. Being stronger it would overcome it and take over Joan, her mind, body, reasoning and desires. In fact the original one was already on the way out although it hadn't realised yet. The new one was not sexually driven but needed power, to be in charge, to take control entirely.

Sofia who was higher than some levels around her usually took charge at times of threat and she called a conference with Maria's angel Vin, and Joan's angel Melba. These two, although not of Sofia's standing had great respect for her having witnessed her powers before. Their charges were at not risk during these meetings for they were capable of conversing while still being in presence, and what to a mere mortal would take ten minutes would be over in a split second on the spiritual plane.

Melba had been aware of the evil infiltration and extra guards had been on stand by to attend at a second's notice. But this new wave brought added problems for there was no justice with them, if they didn't like you that was it, you were destroyed. Vin hadn't been aware of anything immediately threatening Maria but with Dick's habits they had to be on the alert in case anything got attached to him and they knew there was an interest already. Beaty didn't seemed to have been targeted either but this was where Joan could be a carrier so extra care was needed. The guardians would be in constant touch and anything at all that was just a bit suspicious was immediately conveyed to the others.

Amy had finished her morning cleaning work and was gunning for trouble. She was what her mother used to call 'on the turn', and although it wasn't affecting her too much she did have her moments. Her periods had gone a bit haywire then stopped. A bit earlier than she expected but not something you would grieve about in fact she was glad of it because it meant that she could earn a bit of money anytime, that was if she was paid which was why she was going to see Cyn now.

She went home first and got into some casual clothes and without warning the other woman she was coming, now stood on her doorstep ringing the bell. It took a few rings before the door partly opened and Cyn peeped out.

"Oh I guessed it would be you."

She looked exactly what she was and with no make up and her hair all over the place anyone would surely have to be desperate to go with her, and especially pay for the privilege.

Without another word she pulled the door open and disappeared into the lounge with Amy hot on her heels. She wasn't letting this one go.

"You knew I'd come. I said I would." This was no timid person facing her now but someone who was demanding her rights.

"Ok don't go on about it. Where's me fags?"

She fumbled about until she found them and lit up.

"I need a coffee. Makes us one."

She wasn't asking but doing her usual ordering people about bit.

"I didn't come here to make you drinks, I came for my payment which you've got. It's mine."

For the first time Cyn saw the determined look and knew this woman wasn't acting, joking or anything but on a mission.

"You'll have it." She sighed. "Anyone would think I was fleecing you. When have I never paid you? Hmm?"

Amy didn't speak but stood her ground and stared at her. Cyn reached for her bag and pulled out some money careful not to let her see what she had. Pulling a few notes out of it she shoved them towards Amy.

"There take it, and now perhaps you'll shut up about it."

But if she thought that was the end of it she had a shock for Amy smoothed out the notes, counted them and looked at Cyn.

"Fifty quid?"

"Look, they didn't get the amount they expected so they didn't get paid right? That means we got less but where else could you go out and pick that up tax free lady? I bet you've had to work twice as hard for that pittance you've earned this morning."

"You said we got so much a bloke and we had six, that's only…… well it's not three hundred each is it?"

Cyn stood up now.

"Now get this into your thick brain. You didn't have six. I had six you just assisted and were a learner. Even the chap said that. So think yourself lucky to have that."

"And how much did you have?" Amy was still angry.

"What the bleeding hell has that got to do with it? I organise it. I could have done that lot myself with my eyes shut and both hands tied behind my back."

"Thought you had."

The last retort was the final straw.

"Right that's the last time you work with me. You hold me back. Go find your own sodding customers. You won't find many that just want to shake hands but you'll regret it. You'll see."

With that she went to the door, flung it open and screamed at her to get out.

"With pleasure." Amy called over her shoulder when she was safely out of reach.

It was only when she had left that Cyn started taking stock. Had she been foolish? She'd coaxed and nurtured this woman assuming she was too thick to take much in and could use her. But just how much of what she'd told her had she retained? Even more, would she blab?

She pondered for a moment.

"If that had occurred to her she would have used it to extort money from me just to keep her mouth shut. Nah, she's not that clever. Thinks she is but she'll be back."

Quite content with that thought Cyn reluctantly made her own coffee.

By the time she'd finished work, Maria had already arranged with Joan that they would both go to Beaty's again. At first she wasn't sure if she wanted company but she was still reeling, not only from last night's attack but from the revelation that Dick was most likely lying about the week end. She knew her aunt's opinion of him and would be a good ear to lean on but could she stand the 'I warned you' lectures that would follow. It didn't matter if they spoke in front of her mum as she wouldn't be listening to half of it and wouldn't remember anyway.

It was five o'clock when she left work and knew she had least an hour before Dick was due, if he came straight home, so she prepared a cottage pie and left it in the oven. She left a note saying where dinner was and to help himself as she had gone to mum's and would have hers when she got back. Although she could have gone after dinner, the least she saw of him the better and anyway it would make it too late for mum to have her meal. Joan was taking something to be heated up and had asked Maria if she wanted some but she had refused. In fact she wasn't that hungry now as her mind and stomach were churning.

"Hi Mum it's me." She called as she let herself in.

"Is that you Joan?" Came the reply.

"No mum. Maria."

"Oh."

Beaty was fumbling about as though she was looking for something.

"Now what have you lost?" Maria tried to give a light hearted laugh.

"Lost?"

"Yes you look as if you'd lost something again."

"Oh. What?"

"Never mind. Oh here's Aunt Joan with your dinner."

Beaty sat down so whatever it was she may have wanted had gone out of her mind.

"Hello Beaty. Hello Maria." Joan was in before the door could be opened for her. Maria went to greet her and followed her into the kitchen.

"I'll just pop this in the microwave." She unwrapped a dish. Then under her breath asked "How is she today?"

"Only just got here. Thought she'd lost something but seems to have forgotten what it was."

"Oh best way. Probably nothing anyway." Joan seemed to be in the kind of mood that nothing could possibly upset her and Maria couldn't help but feel a bit envious.

"What are you muttering about?"

Beaty called from the lounge.

"Nothing, just coming in." Joan called before her niece could even open her mouth to answer but she held her finger to her mouth to whisper.

"I unplugged the microwave." Maria pointed to it.

Joan looked from her to the oven.

"Why? Oh don't tell me she's cremated something."

"Well she was fiddling with the knobs and I didn't feel she was safe with it."

"No. I think you're right. Well spotted." Joan put the plug in and said "Must remember to always take it out and try and tuck it away so she can't do any damage."

"You are. You're muttering." Came the cry from the lounge.

After putting the dish in and setting the knobs, Joan indicated they go and join Beaty.

"Here we are. We were just sorting out your dinner. How are you?"

Joan had moved the conversation on knowing Beaty had probably already forgotten calling them.

"What day is it?"

"It's Thursday Mum."

"Oh. Are you sure only I could have sworn it was......." She obviously didn't know one day from the next. .

"Doesn't matter," Joan piped up, "we're here now. Dinner won't be long."

"What does the enemy say?" She looked toward the clock.

"It's teatime Mum."

It was easier to identify it by meals that she'd always known than give an exact time which would be forgotten immediately.

"Oh."

"Has anybody been?" Joan knew this was futile but there was little else to talk about where they may get a sensible answer.

"When?"

"Don't worry about it. Anyway it's that time of year again."

The blank stare was expected.

"It comes round so quickly doesn't it? Your annual check up at the doctors." Joan turned to Maria. "I'm due mine as well, that's how I remember."

"What check up? I don't need a check up." Beaty was looking from one to the other.

Maria held her hand.

"It's what they do these days Mum when you get to a certain age. It's called a well person check." She gave a quick glance to her aunt by way of reassurance.

"Yes that's right. Just to make sure everything is ticking over nicely." Joan assured her.

"Do we go together then?"

That could have been tricky but there was the obvious answer.

"We can't. We don't have the same doctor." Joan smiled as she spoke.

"Well I've never heard of it, I'm not ill."

"That's the whole point Mum, we want to keep you that way."

Beaty now turned and looked her full in the face.

"What we always said was If it 'aint broke, don't fix it."

Joan gave a forced laugh.

"Oh Beaty the world's changed since we were young. They don't wait for you to get ill now, they try and forecast it so they treat you before it gets bad."

It was clear that it wasn't going to be easy but they knew that it had to be sooner rather than later or this stubborn old goat would dig her heels in and refuse to go. Fortunately Maria had the same doctor's practice and said she would be with her all the time. Beaty didn't look convinced and they knew that she would have forgotten all about it when the time came and they'd have to start explaining all over again.

"This young man that I work with sees it all the time. He works with elderly people and says what a good idea it is." Joan had to get Frank into the conversation, and not just for Beaty's sake.

"I'll just go and check on the dinner." Maria got up and cast Joan a look which meant she wanted to speak alone.

Once in the kitchen she asked "Will it work?"

"Should do. She'll go along with it, can't do much else."

"I want a word." Maria whispered.

"Oh yes." Joan was waiting for this. "About the bruises?"

"You can't see any." Maria almost mouthed it.

"Don't need to but they're there aren't they?"

"Can we talk in front of Mum?"

"Don't see why not, she won't take much in and she'll forget anything she does hear." Joan shrugged and tried to sound casual.

They were quiet while Joan plated up the meal and although Maria felt guilty getting a medical diagnosis she knew there was no other option. It had come to this, something she had never really thought about and now it was staring her in the face, it was horrible. Not her Mum. It couldn't be happening to her. But inside she knew the truth.

Joan took the dinner in while Maria ran some water in the washing up bowl.

"There you are Beaty, enjoy."

"Has he beaten her up?"

Joan nearly dropped the plate.

"Who?"

"I'm not daft. She's hurt her arm. What's he done?"

Her sister was gobsmacked. How could this person who was three sheets to the wind most of the time have picked that up?

"Just eat your dinner love. She's OK. Honestly."

The look she got back was a chink of light in a dark sky, there for a second but would be gone in a moment. But it proved that what was on the surface could obscure hidden depths at certain times. They would have to be very careful what they discussed now.

As she went back into the kitchen she mouthed to Maria that they must speak when they had left. At first she got a questioning look but it was followed by a nod that confirmed she understood.

They parked in the next street and Maria joined Joan in her car.
"What is it?"
Her aunt gave her a strange look.
"Weird, very weird. You know how she is, I know how she is, it's plain for anyone to see but, you know when I took her dinner in?"
Maria nodded.
"Well," Joan continued "for a fleeting moment she was back then it had gone. We're going to have to be very careful what we say."
"In what way, I mean, you said she was back?"
"Her face remained the same but she asked if he'd beaten you."
"What? Get out. She didn't."
"She did I tell you. Then said you'd hurt your arm."
"What else?"
"That was it, she'd gone back into cloud cuckoo land again."
Maria looked out of the window as if searching for an answer, then back to Joan.
"Is this normal?"
Here was the chance the aunt had been waiting for.
"Hmm. It's no good, I'll have to run all this past Frank, can't put it off."
"Is he qualified in this sort of thing then?"
Joan took a breath as this had to come out casually.
"Frank, he works with the elderly and mental health, all that kind of thing and supports our shop. Lovely man. I told you"
Not wanting any probing questions she continued "I'll have a word with him tomorrow. He's the best one to advise us. He knows what channels you have to go through, it doesn't happen overnight you know."
"What doesn't? Dementia?" Maria seemed to be in a dream.
"No, the system. It has to follow a certain path. I hear about it all the time in the shop."
"Sounds like a plan." Maria was trying to be co-operative but her mind was already going over Dick's excuse for going away.

Before she got out of the car Maria said without looking up "He's going away for the weekend."

"Who Frank? He never said."

"No. Dick. And he's lied about it. I know he has."

"Oh my dear girl why didn't you say before. Well good riddance to bad rubbish I say. Oh I'm sorry, that's not helping is it."

She could see Maria wasn't only physically but mentally in pain.

"Look, why don't you come and stay with me? Be company for us both and I can fuss over you." She gave a very understanding little smile. "And we can go and see your mum together. How about it? Makes perfect sense."

Maria looked up.

"Do you know, I think that would be lovely. Yes please."

"That's settled then. We'll have a girlie weekend."

As Maria went out get out of the car Joan called after her.

"We'll face this together. You mustn't feel alone. I'm here."

"Which bit?" Maria was forced to smile.

"All of it. And when I have a problem you can help me. How does that sound?"

Although it was forced humour it lifted the spirits a little on both sides. Joan was glad to be of some use and her niece knew she wouldn't be fighting these battles alone which makes a huge difference to anyone who is ever in this kind of situation. But one thing was certain, Maria wasn't going to tell Dick.

It was conference time. Sofia was in communication with Melba and Vin about what Joan had up her sleeve for the weekend. They knew that now she would have Maria to herself for a while she could nurture the Frank situation but without realising it was the evil attachment that was spurring her on and they didn't take failure. If they decided they wanted this to happen, it would. They also had a cell working on Frank which was why Joan was coming into his thoughts frequently. They had planned that when he met Maria, and he certainly would, he would be torn between the two and even go for a threesome.

Such was the power of this evil that all his standards would evaporate as his forced emotions took over. It wouldn't matter that Maria was married or how old Joan was, that would be immaterial for he was simply a tool. They used the most unlikely people as carriers so the likes of Joan would never be suspected of having any connection with anything unsavoury and would in turn either be drawn into the currant plan or as was often the case, be let loose to spread it elsewhere. Beaty seemed to be pretty safe as her mind wasn't stable enough to manipulate which was in fact a blessing.

Maria walked into the house thinking "Please don't start." But he wasn't there. She checked the kitchen and saw that he'd had his dinner because the dirty plates were on the working surface, a hand towel strewn the little table and a dirty beaker on the drainer. It seemed as though he had wanted to leave the place as bad as possible after she'd left it clear.

"Oh play your silly games little boy." She muttered, left the room and went up to bed making no attempt to clear up after him.

"Let his floosy do it. Let her clean up when his pumped all over her." She tried to control her anger but she was so tired that tears took over and she fell to the bed sobbing.

After a few moments she pulled herself together and got ready for bed as she didn't want to get into conversation when he finally returned. It was some time before she heard his key in the door. He must have gone into the kitchen and seen that she hadn't bothered to do anything and that should have made him think because she always like a clean place to come down to in the morning. When she heard him coming up the stairs she made sure her face was covered and she had her back to his side of the bed.

"Are you asleep?" He whispered.

As she lay there she couldn't help thinking that if she were, how could she answer?

It seemed to take ages before he finally got into bed and she now looked forward to Saturday when she wouldn't have to share this one. When she came back and more to the point if he came back, she would sort out the spare room and sleep in there as she couldn't bear the closeness of him. Goodness knows where he'd been tonight, and with whom. But worse than that was the fact of the continual lies.

As she lay there a thought came to her. Wouldn't it be funny if she should just happen to bump into his boss that weekend, or even his wife? No knowing where they lived it didn't seem a possibility but you never knew.

The phone rang, too loudly for her liking but Cyn fumbled around for it because it could be more work and she felt she needed something to make up for the last fiasco.

"Yeah?"

"I hope you don't mind my ringing, but I've been given your number." The male voice was very cultured.

"Oh yeah. Who by?"

"Well, shall we just say a friend?"

"Aint got none."

"Oh that's not what I've have been told."

She sat up. Maybe this one had dosh.

"Um, well, sorry I wasn't properly awake."

"Late night I expect."

"You could say that." She lit a cigarette.

"Do you perform all hours?"

She was beginning to wish he'd get to the point but something also made her wonder.

"Depends."

"Well I am very particular, I only like the best."

"I'm sure you do m…." she was going to say mate but it didn't sound right, "Mr…?"

"Well we don't have to bother with preliminaries do we, and you are a very busy lady."

She took a drag on her fag.

"Tell me, just what is it you're looking for?"

"You name it."

He was being quite evasive and a few warning signs lit up. This could be the vice squad watching her after the other night. She thought she'd been careful but you never know. She decided to play the fob off tactic.

"Well now, I do costume jewellery parties, ladies underwear but that would be of no interest to you, and sometimes we have a wig party."

She wasn't ready for what came next.

"Shut up you stupid bitch, you know what I'm after." The voice had changed somewhat. "I can't wait I need help now."

"Then go and choke your chicken somewhere else buster, I'm not here for that." And she threw the phone on the table.

"Filthy bugger wants a free wank. What does he think I am?"

The phone rang again and without checking what number was incoming she grabbed it and yelled "Clear off you filthy jerk or I'll report you."

A familiar voice answered "You having trouble gal?"

"No, I've just had a tosser on, literally."

It was the man who organised the dominance.

"Oh well you can handle them, well not like that." He laughed.

"What-you-want?" She wasn't wasting words and it all came out in a string.

"Look I know you didn't have much fun last time but I got another one. How about it, only there's one problem."

"Which is?" She was thinking that the problem, from her point of view, was the money.

"Well, you gotta do it on your own, I mean they get so much time each and you just have to move 'em through. Now I'm sure you can hack this if you're not held back, if you get me."

"Oh I get you. But lets be honest, this just ain't the big time." Then she added "How many, how long?"

"I got nine. Twenty mins each. You'd walk it in three hours."

"How much?"

"Three hundred the lot."

"What? "

"Like you say this ain't the big time. They'd normally have longer and pay more. And get a professional."

"Oh thanks. And what do you think I am.?"

"Well if you're not interested."

"Double it."

"Four."

"Five."

"Done." He was happy with that. Some of the men may have thought they were paying to high but they wanted anonymity so they got relief in secret.

"Same place." She asked.

"Not this time. Can't risk doing the same one twice. I'll let you know. But on your tod." He emphasised.

"Don't worry. I intend too." She felt relieved not to have Amy tagging along. Doesn't matter what job you do, having a trainee always slows you down.

As it was still too early for her to surface, she stubbed her cigarette out on the nearest thing which happened to be a plate, rolled over and went back to sleep.

Chapter 7

It may have been alright for Cyn to sleep through the day but others had normal day jobs. As Maria got ready for work she was almost looking forward to being on her own, to be precise, away from him. She was beginning to have second thoughts about staying with Joan because the prospect of being totally free for a while, being able to eat what and when she liked, didn't even have to get dressed if she didn't feel like it was a very attractive thought.

"But she'd be so disappointed and we do have to look after Mum." She thought. "Ah well, never mind."

The arse wipe had already left with very few words and had almost acted as though she wasn't there.

"Wish he'd stay wherever he's going." She thought but then added "Who'd have him?"

However she was hatching a little plan of her own.

Joan had offered to pop in to make sure Beaty had got up and dressed and had not fiddled with any more controls and they agreed to both go when Maria had finished work, and all have a meal together. But she was also going to plan today to get Frank over there during the weekend, and as had previously suggested that he would be introduced as a friend. She very carefully didn't go into details in case her niece put her foot down because she smelt a bit of meddling.

Today was going to be quite interesting on many counts.

The lads where Dick worked had been very amused since the fancy bit had chatted him up. She used to come in occasionally but one of the mechanics knew her from where he'd worked before and spread all he knew among the others. Dick had never liked him since he arrived and so the newcomer felt it would be quite amusing if he found out for himself what a man eater she was. He'd forgotten her until she had come into this garage and then he remembered all about her. It was time for a bit of karma, then maybe Dick wouldn't be so cocky after his weekend away.

Nothing was actually said but the air was electric and the looks that were being exchanged soon got to Dick.

"Ok you load of tossers, what's the joke?" He finally threw a spanner on the floor and looked round at them.

"Oooooo." Was chorused in a high pitched girly tone then one called "Got your knickers in a knot?"

"Hope he's been to the barbers." Another muttered just loud enough to be heard.

"Ok. You're all having your jokes now, but you're all jealous. That's what it is. I'm having the fun and you sad bastards will have the same old boring weekend. Well tough."

With that he turned back to the motor he was fixing.

One whispered to another "I'd rather be bored thanks."

Phil came to check on the progress of one of the jobs and clarified who would be in the following morning.

"Well Dick won't that's for sure." One of them couldn't resist having a final poke.

Joan knew how to play people and she was certainly not going to let that talent go to waste, especially now. As soon as she had opened the charity shop she was on the phone.

"Oh Frank I don't know which way to turn." A slight sob was inserted here. "She's getting worse by the minute. We're going to have to get her to the doctors but she's being stubborn and we can't drag her there against her will."

"Calm down," Frank's tone was soothing "look I'm tied up this morning but I could pop round this afternoon. What time do you go?"

"Well, it's about four usually."

"I'll see you before then. Is there anyone else on with you today?"

"Only at lunchtime, she can't do too many hours because of her husband you see."

"Ok, stay calm and we'll talk. I promise."

As she put the phone back on the cradle a little self satisfied smirk crept over her face.

"That's the first hurdle down."

Although she felt in control, she had a lot of back up for the evil were working this to infiltrate the good souls. They didn't worry about those that were on the downward path because they already had them. No, it was those with scruples and high standards they needed to knock off their perches and gather them in. She wouldn't stand a chance any more than that niece of hers.

Something had been niggling at Maria, although with all that was going on she couldn't quite place it. When she accidently overheard a bit of an exchange with the woman working next to her, things began to register. On her coffee break she sat quietly and tried to think of things that had been said.

Vin, her angel guard was firing ideas at her, trying to stimulate her brain into seeing what was going on. The night of Dick's cock bite, for the want of a better description, Amy had phoned her.

Now this was a woman who she had met recently at a local bazaar and they'd got chatting. Maria had felt a bit sorry for her as the poor thing didn't seem to have much push and people appeared to take advantage of her. Being one to protect the under dog she'd seen her a couple of times for a coffee but didn't really want to get too involved. Also she seemed to be a gossip monger so you had to be careful what was said because it could end up anywhere as quite a different story.

With all that had gone on that night, Maria wouldn't have remembered much but with her angel's help, the important things were being brought to the fore and highlighted.

"Just a minute." A beam of distrust was forming. "She phoned that night to say a friend of her Mum's saw Dick's car, or thought she did. And she wanted me to know."

For some reason a terrific doubt was planted.

"She lives near her mum in a small rented place."

Again a prod of information. The light was dawning.

"It wasn't her mum's friend at all. It was her. Yes her mum did live opposite the prostitute. But she didn't have a friend that near as far as she knew, and all that about walking the dog was a load of cobblers. It was Amy that had been snooping and she knew it was Dick's car and couldn't wait to stir the shit.

And then why did she ring to say about Phil? What had that got to do with anything apart from idle gossip. But this tittle tattle was working its way round Maria's mind as the angels wanted it to.

If Dick was going away this weekend with Phil, it was a bit obvious if they were going off to get their ends away. But she had already decided she was going to check the Phil aspect out anyway, and if Joan got onto it as well, there would be no stopping them.

Fortunately, with Amy only being a recent, not so close, friend Maria could take it as a lesson not to be so trusting, but when it's a long term friendship or relationship it goes very deep.

The rest of Friday took its course with little excitement. Joan had been talking to Maria at lunchtime and told her that this nice man Frank would be only too pleased to pop in at Beaty's tomorrow, just as a friend she emphasised again, and see what he could advise.

"Um, who's friend are you saying it is?" Maria had asked.

"Oh mine of course, after all you don't know him do you?"

"That's ok then."

She knew her aunt from old, and just wanted to know where this was going without any complications. It was bad enough with how mum was, and what with the 'Dickhead' fiasco she didn't want anything else to worry about.

"Look I was thinking," Joan had suggested "I can cope tonight, give you a break, you just keep your eye on him and what he packs for the weekend."

She knew her aunt meant well but talk about rubbing it in! But in a way it was tinged with guilt for Joan had this little plot hatching and wanted to keep her sweet or it could all go pear shaped.

"Well alright, if you're sure."

"That's settled then. Now what time are you going to come tomorrow?"

"Um, I hadn't really thought about that yet. What were you thinking?"

"Well," Joan gave a little laugh "as soon as he's cleared off is fine with me. Now, do you want to come here first and dump your stuff then we both go to your mum's or……."

This was getting too organised in a way and Maria really just wanted to chill and take it as it came.

"How about if I went to mum's and made sure she'd had breakfast then came over to yours?"

"Well, I should think that would do."

Joan was obviously disappointed as she felt she wasn't in complete charge and that didn't go down very well.

"Ok, I'll let you know when I'm leaving hers. But there's something I have to do."

"Oh?"

This called for an explanation and it was easier to come out with it than hedge round it for ages.

"I'm just going to check out his story that's all."

"Oo that sounds good. What are you going to do?" Joan loved the sound of this.

"Simply pop by the garage and see if Phil's there."

Joan liked this. "On what pretence may I ask?"

"Oh I won't actually ask for him but say....um."

"You haven't thought this through have you?"

"I'd just ask one of them to check one of my tyres and say something like 'I'd get Dick to do it but he's away' and see what they say."

"Oh my dear girl." Her aunt laughed. "Leave it to me."

"What, but......"

"If he's up to something, they could all know, men brag dear. Do you want them laughing behind your back?" Without waiting for a reply she answered herself. "Of course you don't."

There seemed no option but actually it was a good idea and knowing Joan, she would come back with the info, and Maria knew she was only trying to help in her way.

"You're right, as usual."

They both laughed and agreed to chat when Joan had done the visit that evening.

Dick had made few calls to his conquest, Zena and they knew they were in for a good time. She put his mind at ease about having her mum and boy friend in tow and reassured him again that they would have plenty of fun time without interruption. So it was agreed he would drive from home as if going to leave his car at Phil's, but would actually park it round the back of where he worked then walk the short distance to the little park where she would pick him up about 9.30am. It was only about an hour's drive to the cottage so they would soon be doing what all the lads at work knew he would be doing. She had so taken over his mind that he was thinking of very little else.

Nobody mattered except his happiness now. According to him life had thrown its share of shit at him so why shouldn't he enjoy what came along. He didn't owe anyone anything so it was about time he put himself first. His ungrateful nature pushed aside the years his wife had worked to help provide enough for their children, go on holiday, look after him when he was ill. All that meant nothing. His selfish side had nearly ended their marriage and lost him no end of friends but he would never change. After each episode there was always the sob story that it was someone else's fault, never his. He was on rock bottom and if anyone was soft enough to offer him help he always used his stock phrase "It really is appreciated" which was as shallow as a puddle.

He never even considered that this would be the final straw as far as Maria was concerned. Oh she may have one of her moments and made idle threats but he would keep saying "I've told you, I'm not going anywhere." He wouldn't believe the times she wished he had.

He hoped that she would be going to her mum's this evening to give him privacy as to what to put in his overnight bag. He'd made sure he'd got a good supply of johnnies just in case. Being summer and decent weather at the moment he wouldn't need much and the last thing he wanted was for his misses to be watching what he put in. But the thought came to him that he was supposed to be going to decent company so had to make it look respectable if she did have a nose through when he wasn't looking. No problem. He could always leave stuff in the car if necessary.

The protective angels were on full alert. With the evil cells working their way into the various individuals they knew they had to halt it now or the ones they were supposed to be protecting would turn on their own guardians and fight back wrongly believing it was all their own desire and not one planted in them.

Sofia wasn't too concerned about Beaty at the moment as she didn't seem to be attracting too much attention but that didn't mean she didn't need constant attention for it's often the most unlikely that can be targeted.

Melba however was aware that the evil was taking root in Joan although it would not be immediately obvious but she still called for back up so that it was in place ready.

Although Maria didn't appear to be a target for any personal reasons, her contact with Joan and Dick made her very vulnerable for if both evil attachments turned and concentrated on her it could be fatal.

In cases like this, the angels knew that devious plans were always being put into operation and quite often people would appear to be possessed by evil but it was a decoy and the bad forces would merely be using them as a waiting area while they observed their actual prey. Therefore the protective shields must be on continual full strength.

Cyn looked in the mirror. She was looking at least ten years older than she really was. She was always hoping for the big time but everyone knew that would never happen. Sometimes she even fancied her clients but they always went as soon as they'd had their relief leaving her alone, again. Her relationships had never worked and the thought of ending up with a decent chap was a pipe dream, but on weighing it up he needn't be all that decent, as long as he was ok and loved her.

"Love?" She was looking in the mirror. "Who'd love that?" It was quite depressing. She didn't know a trade, apart from her own and had moved about a bit when one area had become boring. She always wanted fresh faces, and other bits of course and the hope that one day she just might be earning what she was worth.

"Wake up dearie." One man had told her "You're from the gutter and that's where you'll always be. You just aint got class."

He ended up in A & E with most unusual injuries but wouldn't say where, how or why he got them.

Amy came into her mind.

"What a drag. Is that all there is to work with, and this being a respectable area as well?"

The phone broke into her thoughts.

"Yeah."

"Hey baby I'm back in town. How's about you and me make some music?"

"Wow you bastard, where you been?"

"Oh just taken a couple of years vacation, but I'm ready for action."

She knew who it was instantly. Not a bad client when he wasn't banged up and she could do with the dosh.

"Well are you gonna get your ass over here?"

There was silence.

"You still there?" She wondered if he'd gone.

"Yeah, just thinking. You got any wheels?"

"Course. Why?"

"Well it would kind of fit in if you could get me."

"Ok where?"

She had the feeling he wasn't alone as he always tried to put on a kind of slow drawl when he was trying to impress. There was a long pause and she was about to hang up.

"Place has changed a bit. Not too sure."

She heard the distinct sound of a kiss.

"Look," she said, "it really isn't good for me tonight. Some other time eh?"And ended the call.

"Cheeky bugger." She exploded. "He's with a tart and is trying to book me? Find yourself another mug mate."

Although she never refused money, she wasn't in the mood for being used like a dirty rag. The evil hangers on were bringing her emotions down to despair level, and those feelings would then turn into absolute hatred of everyone and eventually become revenge. When someone already has those traits in their make up, any encouragement is seized and taken on board so watch out anyone who gets in their way.

Amy was feeling a bit lost. Although Cyn was winding her up with her attitude, without her she felt unprotected and didn't know where her next little job was coming from. She wondered whether to ring her but felt she couldn't risk the kind of response she could get. The woman had been getting very temperamental of late and Amy was wishing someone else would take her place but she didn't have many friends and you couldn't very well just walk up to someone and ask if they could get you that kind of job. Her mind slipped to Maria.

"I wonder if she knows anyone." She mused. "After all I do tell her all that's going on, and she wouldn't know about Dick if I hadn't said so I I'm doing her a favour really."

This poor creature began to feel that Maria now owed her one. But the playful spirits were feeding her these ideas to stir things up for their amusement and she was a prime candidate.

"I'll ring her in a bit." She decided. "Now what can I tell her that she'd really want to know?"

Nothing seemed to come to mind and she'd already said about Phil, so there was nothing else for it. She'd have to make something up.

The day seemed to drag for most people in different ways but eventually for those at work it was knocking off time.

For Beaty one hour was much like the rest now and although she spent a lot of time trying to work out what part of the day it was, it didn't help much. Joan had just arrived but she wasn't sure if she was bringing breakfast or dinner.

"What does the enemy say?"

This kind of repeated remark gets to many family members but Joan was on too much of a high for it to bother her.

"It's just gone six Beaty, and I've got you a lovely dinner. Your favourite."

"Oh thank you. What is it?"

"Steak and kidney pie, and you've got trifle for afters."

"You haven't done tons have you only I can't eat big meals these days."

Joan brought the plate in and put it on the laptray.

"Oh will you take a look at that?" Beaty looked all over the plate smiling.

"I'm just going to get you a drink and then I'll be right back."

Joan realised that she might as well have already left the room but kept the smile on her face. She'd heard of this change in behaviour and even seen it in others but when it's not an older relative but your younger sister, it takes on a whole new meaning. And it would get steadily worse. Any conversation would be forgotten in minutes which was almost the case now, but she would still tell her about Frank knowing full well she wouldn't remember the next day, so she would keep repeating it. Eventually it would be very wearing but she'd cross that bridge when she came to it.

Beaty had eaten quite a bit and said she was 'stodged'.

Joan laughed. "Well you should sleep well tonight then."

"I could nod off now."

"Go on, I'm not stopping you."

"Better not or I shan't sleep when I get to bed."

A little bell went off in Joan's head. Did she actually go up to bed?

"Just going to the loo." She called as she went upstairs.

The bed was as she had made it but she turned the corner back so that she would notice if it had been moved when she came the next day. Also she made a mental note of what clothes she had on although that didn't necessarily tell her anything as Beaty could have washed herself and put the same ones back on.

As she went back into the lounge Beaty was already asleep. It seemed a shame to wake her, and if she started telling her anything, she wouldn't be with it enough to remember. Making sure everything was safe, she drew the curtains and put the lamp on the side table on low and quietly locked up and left the house. It would be light for quite a while yet but if her sister woke up in the dark she might panic and fall.

As she went home she made a decision. She would have to come round in the morning to check the bed and everything else, so she would definitely be there when Maria came.

Cyn was looking at her phone. Her moods were swinging like a pendulum and at this moment she was lonely. Should she ring the silly bitch? Was she that desperate? Who else could she call? As if by magic it rang. Even the ringtone was getting on her nerves and she knew she must change it.

"Yeah."

Silence. Cyn listened for the inevitable heavy breather and was about to tell them what a filthy piece of shit they were when the call was cut off. She was about to throw it down in temper but her brain told her to check the recent call list. She didn't recognise the number. Thinking that it was either missed business or a wrong number she swore under her breath and reached for a drink.

A few minutes later it rang again, same number. This time she hit the button but didn't speak. After a few seconds it was cancelled again.

"What the bloody hell is going on?" She fumed and made up her mind that if it happened again she would just let it ring. This put her on edge. Will it? Won't it? After about five minutes it went, same number. Against her better judgment she grabbed it and yelled at it, holding it about a foot from her as though she was speaking to someone face to face.

"Now look here whoever you are, do you want something or not? But if you've got something to say, stop pissing about and get on with it. If not, bugger off."

"I'm so sorry. I didn't want to disturb you." It was a man's voice and he sounded petrified.

"Who is this? What do you want?"

She didn't expect what happened next. A low laughter was coming down the phone and it was sinister.

"What do I want? Oh I don't want anything. I'm just doing my job."

"Look you sick pervert, go and annoy somebody else." She was getting angry. Someone must have given her number to this person who was either demented or had a funny way of asking her for service.

"You've got it all wrong, I'm not sick. I'm just doing my job."

"You've just said that. Now either say what you want or……."

"Aren't you even interested? You should be. I would be if I was being watched 24/7."

Now she sat up. This wasn't like anything she'd ever had before. It was usually someone who had been recommended, or someone trying to sell something or the sprinkling of dirty calls, but this had a very different feel to it.

"Who is this? And you'd better come clean, do you hear?"

"Oh you'll find out soon enough. But remember, we are watching, wherever you go and whatever you do."

"Oh yeah, too right. Think you can scare me like that? Sod off."

The next words froze her to the spot.

"Don't spill anything on the nice little green cushion, and isn't it time that ashtray was emptied? Not sure about that nail polish though."

With that he'd gone.

Her first thought was to look round the room. Someone must have been in and put a camera somewhere while she was out. Then she thought of what he'd said. If he was looking at her cushion and the coffee table the camera must be over that side of the room. For some reason she then wondered if he was sitting outside in a vehicle but not wanting to look out of the lounge window, she ran upstairs and looked from her bedroom. There were the usual cars in the street but no sign of any other and nobody was hanging about. She went back downstairs and looked around the room which would provide a view of her sofa area but there seemed to be nothing.

She was really freaking out and automatically lit a cigarette and reached for a strong drink then went to sit back on the sofa but changed her mind. What if she was being watched?

"Oh this is bloody ridiculous." She was so wound up she felt she'd explode. He was kidding. How could anyone have put a camera in here? And why would they want to? Except some pervert wanting a free show?

That was it. One of her blokes must have rigged it so they could watch her with a customer, but why downstairs, why not the bedroom? But then she had shagged men on the sofa, so that was it. It had to be one of those. She sat racking her brain as to who had visited recently but it had been a while because she always preferred to go out, away from home. Then it hit her. It was when Amy was here and those two builders came, and she was downstairs with hers while Cyn was upstairs. At least they said they were builders, they could have been anybody.

"I don't need this. All I want is to pay my bills and have a bit extra for myself. What's wrong with that?" She sat for a long time pondering over it but from then on felt she was looking over her shoulder all the time wondering who was watching.

Amy was washing up when a knock came at the door. It was someone she'd met at work and had been getting quite chatty with. He'd started by just making small talk then it became a bit more in depth until, under the pretence of being interested in her extra curricular activities got her to be quite informative as to her general way of life.

She had been telling him how Cyn was really getting on her nerves and she didn't like the controlling part. Being a very kind person, he said quite casually that that kind of behaviour should be nipped in the bud or she would have no will of her own. That she would be doing everything this woman wanted and have no say in the matter and she wouldn't be able to stop it. He tried to keep it in simple language so that she knew exactly what he was saying.

"Oh I wouldn't like that." She had confided.

"Then do something about it."

"I wouldn't know how."

Here was his chance.

"No, but I would."

" Really. How?" She couldn't believe she was hearing this.

"You just leave that side of it to me." Was all he would say with one of his boyish grins.

Now he was at her front door because she had told him where she lived, and where Cyn lived and he had both their phone numbers.

"How did it go?" She couldn't wait to ask as he stepped over the thresh hold.

"Like a dream. She'll be a nervous wreck before long." He made his way into the lounge and let her follow.

"What did she say?" Amy was bursting with excitement because Cyn would never guess she had been at the bottom of the prank. Well not at the bottom as she hadn't that much brain but cheering it along.

"Not a lot she could say but she was really gobsmacked I can tell you. Bet she crapped herself."

"Oh I wish I could have seen it." Amy was almost jumping up and down.

He was now sitting on the small sofa and was taking off his thin jacket.

"Perhaps I should have fixed a camera up then." He jested. "Like watching as well do you?"

His tone had changed and for the first time Amy began to feel a bit uncomfortable.

"Um would you like a cup of tea?"

He completely ignored the offer and said "It's settling up time."

She was hovering nervously not quite sure what he meant.

"Well nothing is for nothing, you know that."

"I-I-I-m, not sure what you mean."

The sad part was she didn't. She'd always followed orders but rarely thought things through for herself.

"Look love, I did something for you and now you do something for me. And don't pretend you don't know what I'm talking about because you've done plenty of it, you told me remember?"

"Yes but that was for……"

"Payment. Of course. And what do you think this is? Let me spell it out so you know. It's called payment in kind."

"You mean……."

"Hooray. You've got it so let's not waste time love, I haven't got all night."

"No. You can't." She screamed. "We didn't say it was like that."

"Oh come on, you know what it's all about, don't come the little innocent with me," he paused inches from her face holding her arms by her side "or you will be sorry, very sorry."

She struggled but he was too strong for her but she seized the moment when he tried to unzip his fly and whip his bollard out. Freeing her self she rushed into the kitchen, grabbed a knife and as he came at her she brought it down with such a force it missed him by about a millimetre. A fraction more and his bollard would have been on the floor. He shoved her so hard she fell at the side of one of the units and he got out while he could.

She lay on the floor shaking and it was only when she heard her next door neighbour's voice she tried to get up.

"I'm in here."

The woman came in and asked her what had happened. They'd seen a man run out leaving the door open and wondered if she had been hurt, or worse.

"Did he attack you love?" She helped her up.

"He was going to rape me."

"Oh."

The neighbour was a bit wary now as everyone round there knew of her association with Cyn and it was common knowledge what she was. This neighbour now worried that it was on her own doorstep.

Checking that Amy wasn't hurt and assured she didn't want to report anything, she went off to let her husband know what had happened. Before she could get to her door, others had come to see what was going on and some were getting a bit fed up with how this area was going. They'd had time for Amy but if she was going to attract this sort, something needed to be done about it.

"It's all that Cyn woman's fault," one complained "it was alright round here till she moved in."

"We don't want it."

"We're not having it."

The women were all in agreement and it didn't help when one of the husbands added "No but some lucky blighters are."

Her comments as he was marched home can only be left to the imagination.

But that was not the end of the incident. It was revenge time.

The phone rang and Cyn just looked at it. Another number she didn't recognise. Curiosity won and she answered.

"Yeah."

"This is a friend. Just thought you'd like to know who was behind the little joke. You aren't on camera. But who knows what you have in your house and where it is?"

"Hang on that could be several people." She was angry at having been fooled. "If you know, just tell me."

"All I will say is……it wasn't of the male sex."

The call had ended.

She sat for a moment then it hit her. "Amy! You disgusting pile of pigshit!" She screamed. If she was livid before it was nothing to what she was now, and the evil that was spurring her on couldn't wait to steer her to the next encounter.

Chapter 8

Dick was fidgeting. He'd relied on Maria going out and now she was under his nose he felt most uncomfortable having her hovering around. It was almost as if she knew something but who could have told her?

He decided on his previous plan, and while she was flitting in and out of the bedroom on the excuse of gathering up washing, he put all the things in the case she would expect. These would be left in the boot of the car before he met Zena.

"You're only stopping overnight." Maria said quietly as she left the room her dislike of him growing by the minute.

While she was almost relieved not to have to visit her mum for an evening, she had an uneasy feeling about Joan's eagerness to please. It was always when she went into overdrive that you knew she was cooking something up. For some reason Frank came into her mind and she really wished that the meeting hadn't been arranged. With all that was going on with Dick she didn't need any added complications. It did cross her mind that Joan may have the hots for a younger man in which case she wished her aunt would keep it to herself and not bring him into the equation.

As soon as Dick was happy Maria was safely downstairs, he texted Zena. It hadn't occurred to him that she may not turn up for this was a dead cert if ever there was.

"Hello gorgeous." He usually opened with that.

"Hi handsome. Missed me?"

"Of course. Can't wait for tomorrow."

"I'm already oozing in anticipation."

"Oh you've got me hard now."

"And what are you going to do about that?"

"Can't. I'm not alone."

There was a slight pause before she replied.

"Don't worry, I'll take good care of it."
"Can't wait." He was trying to subside but it wasn't working.
With the usual hearts and kisses she'd gone.

What should he do? If he went to the bathroom, Maria would undoubtedly time it to come up at that moment. No good he'd just have to think of something to put him of for now.

The next morning dawned with the promise of being very interesting for many parties.

Cyn was gunning for Amy but she wasn't going to move until she'd really thought it through and when she had finished with her, the woman wouldn't be fit to even look at a bloke let alone service him.

Amy on the other hand really thought she had got one over on Cyn little knowing the whistle had been blown, so she felt very smug and was going to start demanding rather than asking.

The guardians of these two were both fighting to keep their charges in line but the evil which had been floating round Cyn for years was growing and now had a new opponent. While Amy's angels had managed to protect her fairly well, her recent activities had attracted a new source which was in opposition to Cyn's followers. So there were now two evil groups who were about to go into battle using their own pawns. The existing ones thought there was no contest for the newcomers were as naïve as their host so Cyn's demons would outwit Amy's without even trying. The angels were well aware of this plan and summoned up extra guards.

Sofia was also right up to date on this latest situation and knew extra back up was needed due to Maria's connection with her so called 'friend'. Fortunately the tactics already put into place by Vin were working, for Maria was certain Amy had been lying and things would be very different from now on.

Joan was up early and in fine spirits. This should be the day when her little scheme came to fruition and she could hardly wait to get round to Beaty's to get it going. She checked the spare bedroom again. Yes everything was perfect for her niece. There was nothing left to do so she was killing time, checking and rechecking and going over what was going to be said, and what if this, and perhaps that. The silly part of it was that probably none of it would go how she thought and at the end of today she would either be elated or extremely disappointed.

Maria was going to mum's for about nine o'clock and Dick beat her out of the house by leaving just after half past eight. He seemed in good spirits which only reinforced her ideas that this was nothing more than a dirty weekend.

"See you tomorrow night love."

Although he kissed her on the lips, his eyes avoided coming into direct contact with hers which again stank of guilt. She was tempted to tell him to have a good time but instead just told him she'd see him tomorrow without asking what time he would be back. To be honest she wasn't even interested, just didn't like being taken for a mug.

He gave a sigh of relief when he was safely round the corner and was on his way to the garage. Now he would have decent sex, all weekend if necessary.

"Hope my cock holds up." He thought. Although it was much improved, there was still a bit of tenderness to cope with but he was sure that if she did the job properly he would be so ecstatic he wouldn't mind a bit of pain.

As he pulled into the entrance of the garage yard, there was just enough space to leave his car without obstructing the gates and as it was off the road there were no parking restrictions. So this would be its home for a couple of days. Going through his bags he discarded some of the items and packed the rest into the larger of the two, leaving the other out of sight in the boot. He knew some of the lads would already be in and wanted to avoid seeing them. Just as he was trying to creep away unnoticed a whistling could be heard coming from the premises. It was 'The Stripper' followed by a few hoots of laughter.

It didn't take him long to get to the little park and he knew he was early but for the first time he wondered if she would turn up. What if this had been a huge joke and the lads all knew about it, or even worse, they could even have set it up by getting her to arrange it. And then what would he say if he had to go back home? Oh, he'd make some excuse about Phil or his wife not being well enough, that wouldn't be the problem.

When you are waiting, a few minutes seem like hours but just before nine a car pulled up beside him. He didn't recognise it at first, it was much larger than the one Zena had driven but she got out of the back seat and took his bag and put it in the boot.

"We're in the back." She took his hand and ushered him into the seat, told him to move up and got in beside him. She pointed to the woman in the front passenger seat.

"This is my mum but she likes to be called Luce."

"Hello Luce." He almost whispered for when she turned he got a shock. Talk about overdoing the make up and surely that was a wig. He hadn't noticed as they pulled up but he sure noticed now.

"Hello Richard." The voice was, to say the least unexpected.

"Um, my name is Dixon." He felt he had to correct her.

"But he's Dick really." Zena chirped.

"Oh I'm sure he is." The undertone couldn't be mistaken and Dick hoped she wasn't going to be coming on to him all weekend.

"And this is her friend, Josh." Zena indicated to the driver.

"Hi Dick." Now that voice was more what he expected.

As they got settled, belted up and drove off Dick couldn't help but wonder what on earth the man saw in the mother. She was gross to put it mildly and if Zena was going to look like that when she was older, he'd back off now.

They'd barely set off before Zena's hand was across to Dick's leg and although it was very enjoyable he didn't like that much company in situations like this. He put his hand on top of hers and mouthed 'later' then cast a glance to the front seats. She smirked but didn't move her hand. The next hour would test him to the limits at this rate.

When Maria got to her mum's she was surprised to see Joan's car already there.

"So much for plans." She thought and hoped the whole week end wasn't going to be too regimental. She needed to relax and still wished she could have had the time on her own at home. But when Joan decided something that was it, she switched off so no matter what anyone said, if she didn't want to hear it, she didn't.

"It's me Mum." Maria called as usual.

"We're in here dear." Joan didn't give Beaty chance to speak.

"Well, I feel redundant." She couldn't help saying as she looked around.

Mum was washed and dressed in clean clothes sitting eating her breakfast.

"I'll get you a cup of tea." Joan stood up.

"I'm alright at the moment thanks."

"You can always do with a cuppa."

It was obvious Joan wanted Maria in the kitchen because you couldn't miss the glances and the nods so she had no option but to follow.

"Wanted to speak to you, but not in front of her." She whispered.

"What is it?" Maria wondered.

"It's as I thought. She doesn't go to bed."

"Oh?"

"I set a trap. She hadn't touched the bed and this morning she was sitting in the chair where I'd left her still in the same clothes."

"Was she wet?" Maria immediately thought that she must have needed the toilet.

"No. I think she may have used the downstairs loo but she's not been up, I'll swear it."

They were quiet for a moment as it was obvious things were changing rapidly. Their thoughts were interrupted.

"What are you two whispering about?" Was called form the lounge.

"We'd better not both go back together or she'll think we've been talking about her." Joan waved her hand for Maria to stay where she was and went out of the kitchen.

"Well we have." Maria thought as she looked round at the tidy place. Just how much had her aunt done since she got here?

Little did she put it down to the fact that Joan had to keep busy to stop her mind dwelling on her other scheme.

She joined them in the lounge.

"Did you enjoy that?" She asked.

"What?" Beaty looked bemused.

"Your breakfast."

"Eh?"

She went to take the tray but Joan was already there.

"Well you must have enjoyed it Beaty, it's all gone." And took everything out to the kitchen.

Beaty beckoned Maria to come a bit closer.

"She's a fusspot."

Maria laughed. "I think she's just trying to look after you Mum."

"Never changed. Always the same." Was the reply.

Sitting on the floor now at her knee Maria looked up as she always had done as a child.

"Did she always boss you about?"

"What? Our mum had to give her a clip round the ear many a time for her bullying me."

"Oh dear, but at least she knew." Maria was loving this. All the memories from way back were still there.

"Ah but the crafty little cow did it behind her back and if I snitched I got told off, because you didn't tell tales."

"Life was very strict then, wasn't it?"

Beaty sighed. "Yes, I suppose it was but you see we didn't think anything of it because that's how we were brought up. That's how life was, you didn't question it."

"Kids today get off lightly don't they?" Maria laughed.

"What? They don't know they're born, they don't."

How long this would have gone on they wouldn't know as Joan reappeared.

"Now, are you listening?" She stood in front of her.

"Can't you sit down, it makes my neck ache looking up." Beaty complained.

Joan didn't like being interrupted but sat in the chair opposite.

"As I was saying, a friend of mine is coming round this afternoon for a chat."

"Who?"

"I'm bringing a friend to see you, for us all to meet, Maria hasn't met him yet either."

"Oh a fancy man. Bit old for that aren't you."

Maria couldn't stifle a laugh. Joan was a bit surprised but thought it a good train of thought so that her sister wouldn't suspect she was being scrutinised.

"Well we'll see. I mean we are only friends at the moment."

"Friends. Huh. Heard that one before." Beaty sniffed then came out with one of her gems. "Not pregnant again are you."

Whether or not her brain was functioning when she said it was anyone's guess but the delivery was priceless.

"Of course not. Don't be silly."

Joan wished they'd keep to the matter in hand but Maria knew that if she kept pushing it her mum may dig her heels in and not want him to come.

"Well I look forward to meeting your friend." She said to her aunt to keep everything on a positive note.

"Who's coming." Beaty asked Maria.

"Aunt Joan is bringing a gentleman friend for us to meet. Mum."

"Oh."

She'd forgotten already so by the time he came they'd have to explain all over again.

Maria thought to herself "Hope she doesn't ask her if she's pregnant while he's here."

When they were safely outside Joan mouthed to Maria. "You go on to mine, I've just got that little detour to do."

"There's no need to whisper, she can't hear you from the house." It was amusing for a moment but them Maria remembered what her aunt was planning.

"Ah you're going to the garage. Well I may as well come too."

"Oh no dear, that would be far too obvious. You pop along now."

Feeling like a naughty child that had been given her orders, there was little choice but to comply.

"When she's got her mind set there's no moving her." She thought as she drove off. The start to the day was obviously a guide to how the next couple of days were going to be. Today was planned but what of tomorrow?

Joan didn't go marching in the front door to the workshop as her niece expected. She knew of the back entrance and guessed what Dick would possibly do. She had estimated he couldn't leave the car in the yard or he wouldn't be able to get it back until the Monday morning because it would all be securely locked. So the only other option was to leave it almost out of sight but accessible. Some of her own antics in her younger days proved very useful which it was why it wasn't that easy to put one over on her.

She drove slowly down the back street and stopped just short of where Dick's car was parked.

"There it is!"

She felt almost smug satisfaction as she realised how blatant he was. Had she been in his position, nobody would have found her vehicle. She didn't need any more proof so didn't have to let any of the mechanics know she was there. It proved that if Dick had been driving Phil, the car would have been parked at the man's house, not tucked away here.

She was home in no time.

"Well?" Maria got out of her car and greeted her.

"Inside." Was all she got.

Safely away from prying eyes and ears, Joan took Maria's little holdall from her and beckoned her to follow her upstairs.

"Here we are."

"Aunt Joan. What did you find out?"

"Um? Oh it's there alright, tucked round the back."

Maria wanted to be sure on the facts.

"So his car is at the back of the garage. But did you speak to anyone?"

"No need dear. Says it all." She was busying about almost avoiding making a conversation out of it.

"You are a devious old goat."

"Me, no. I just put two and two together and usually come out with the right answer. Now, we have to get lunch then talk about this afternoon."

When they were sitting in the lounge, that is Maria was sitting and Joan was buzzing about like a bee, her niece asked just what was so important about this Frank person.

"It's always better to get information from someone you know. Can't get fobbed off then you see." Joan was holding the conversation without making eye contact.

"Knowing you, I just get a feeling that you are plotting again."

"Me dear, now why would I want to do something like that? Now where did I put those tissues? Oh here they are, little devils."

"Aunt Joan."

"Yes dear." There was still no lull in the movement.

"Aunt Joan. Will you sit down for a moment and talk to me without doing, I mean fussing about."

She wouldn't normally have been so blunt but with all that was going on she felt her head was spinning and she needed to be in a calm atmosphere not one that might explode at any moment.

"Well there's a lot to think about."

"No, there isn't. Look I'm sorry but I am like a coiled spring and I thought this was going to be relaxing and I could at least chill for a moment."

The retort was harsh and brought Joan to a standstill. She put the things on the table and sat at the side of Maria.

"Look, I know what you're going through and it isn't easy, but that's what I'm here for."

The evil surrounding Joan was about to stir things up even more.

She continued. "You see, you're just sitting back and taking all the rubbish he throws at you without doing anything about it. But that's where you're wrong. You've got to give as good back as he's giving you. Come on, be honest, what is he making you feel like?"

"I know one thing, I'm on a knife edge and I don't know how much more aggro I can take."

"Exactly, and where do you think you will end up?" Joan sat back, her lips pursed and a very knowing look on her face.

"Like I said, I need to be calm, but everything around me is winding me up, Mum, him and….."

"You were going to say me weren't you?"

"I don't know, I don't know." Maria was ready to walk out of the door and just keep walking, anywhere it didn't matter. "I don't think you realise just what it's like."

"Oh, I do I can assure, I've been there."

If anybody had known any stress, Joan would have had it ten times worse. Everything had to be bigger and better. But she wasn't ready for Maria's next bullet.

"Have you ever cut a bloke's cock off?"

That stopped her dead in her tracks. Joan's mouth was hanging open as she stared in silence.

"No, I thought not. Well I was ready to do it the other night, until he came home, like he did, you know all bitten. I should have finished the job while I was at it, but shall I tell you something? It gave me greater satisfaction watching him squirm in pain. For once I was in charge."

"Well.... Um... the moment has passed and you didn't did you? So that means you couldn't if it came to it." Joan was almost rambling.

"Oh ho, believe me I could. Everyone has their breaking point and I'm damned well near mine. Which is why I don't want you throwing any new problems into the mix. Do you get me?"

"Loud and clear dear. Loud and clear."

There was silence for a moment then Joan found her second wind.

"Well it's good that's all out. You'll feel better now, you mark my words."

Maria had the feeling that not a word had been taken on board and whatever scheme aunt had planned for today, nothing was going to stop her, so it may be best to keep quiet and let it all roll over her head. But the evil was determined it would be very different.

Amy was about to finish her morning job and was just getting her things together.

"Hello."

The man's voice made her swing round.

"Yes?"

She was very wary after the last encounter she'd had with a man at this place and didn't want to go through that again.

"You're Amy, am I right?"

"I've got to go, can't be late." She tried to walk past him.

"Just a minute, you haven't heard what I've got to say."

"Well perhaps I don't want to hear. You men are all alike."

"Oh please don't judge one person by another. We're not all bad you know." He was walking with her to the door.

"I should be going. I've got some shopping to do."

"Great, I'm off for lunch now so we'll talk as we go. Ok?"

She really didn't want to speak to him but he seemed quite nice so perhaps it wouldn't hurt to just hear what he had to say, but she wouldn't tell him anything about herself, where she lived or give him her phone number.

"Well, what did you want?" She asked while looking straight ahead.

"It's just that I might be able to help you."

"Oh I don't think so." She said, then asked "In what way? Help I mean."

"Well I've heard from a good friend of mine that you do a good job and you are very reasonable."

"If you're saying what I think you're saying you can piss off."

"Now don't be too hasty until you've heard what I'm offering."

She stopped and faced him.

"I know your sort and I don't want to hear what you or anybody else is offering. Get me?"

She walked on muttering under her breath about men thinking she was a push over, taking advantage etc.

"Look, Amy. It's not me. It's my brother, he can get you some work. Now don't tell me you don't need the money."

"Oh so you go looking round for business for him do you? And what made you think I'd be interested?"

"But you do it for that tart you call a friend."

"Oh her. Hey wait a sec. How do you know about that?"

"Sweetheart, when you are in that line, everyone knows. Now why not just let him get you one job and if you don't like it you needn't do another. Simple as that."

"You mean, I would be free to go my own way? No ties like?"

"Free as a bird. Free as a bird."

He knew he'd picked a right one because the likes of Cyn would have either jumped at it or told him exactly where he could get off in her usual colourful way leaving him in no doubt whatsoever.

"Well it would be useful. But nobody scruffy."

"You leave it all to my brother. Now I will be your contact."

"I'm not giving my phone number, not again, nearly got me dead."

He laughed.

"Don't worry, it will all be by little messages. Only I will have it."

"But your brother is….."

She needed it spelling out.

"Yes my brother will arrange it and I will give you the details. You don't meet him, he doesn't meet you. No phone calls or any contact with him whatsoever. That's the way he works. Do you understand?"

"Oh yes that sounds very good. Um...."

"Yes?"

"What about the pay, you know the dosh?"

"Well my brother charges the customer and then I bring you your bit."

"Oh." Her mind flashed back to the night of the dom party.

"Is that a problem?"

"Well before, I mean I didn't get it straight away and then, well..."

Somebody ripped her off he thought but assured her "This isn't back street business my love. You will get paid and what you are worth. Time to start living."

With that he had gone leaving her a bit bewildered. Her first instinct was to ask Cyn if it sounded alright but she wouldn't be speaking to her for a while and anyway she would want to muscle in on it and Amy wasn't having that. This could be a new start and she walked on feeling there was hope for her yet.

The journey to the cottage seemed further than Dick imagined but mainly because Zena was making it very difficult for him and being so obvious that everyone in the car would know what was going on. They turned down a small road and travelled about a mile before turning again into a private wooded lane which led down to their destination.

Dick looked ahead with this mouth open. For there stood a small but elegant country manor house.

"You said it was a cottage."

"Well it is of sorts. I mean it's not the main abode but it does for little visits like this."

"You'll be telling me it's full of servants next." He was having serious doubts about this.

"Don't be silly, only a couple but they don't live in."

"That must be the gardener." He noticed a young man on a motor mower.

"One of his lads. It takes a lot keeping this place ship shape you know."

"I can imagine." He was still in shock. "And who else?"

"Oh just the cook of course and a couple of maids. But they'll be gone after dinner."

Dick now wished he'd known about this as his meagre wardrobe would look exactly what it was. Working class among the rich. He'd have got something more in keeping but there was nothing he could do about it now and she had told him not to take too much.

They pulled up at the front door and a young lad came out to carry the bags.

"Well he can't be a maid." Dick thought. "So how many more are there?"

As they went into the house it was obvious it wasn't lived in permanently for the place smelled very musty and had an air of emptiness about it. So why keep it?

Zena answered the unspoken question.

"Bit of a drag really, but you just can't sell these places you know. Would be better as a school or hospital or something. Had a few look at it so you never know. I'd miss the old place, it's so handy for getaways if you know what I mean."

She'd sidled up to him and almost had her hand in his trouser pocket. It seemed funny that the other two took no notice whatsoever of them and seemed to be eager to get to their room as quickly as they could.

"They must all be desperate round here." He thought to himself.

The strange thing was that when he was taking the reins while having sex he was ok, but here he wasn't in charge and it didn't feel right. He just hoped he could perform when push came to shove.

The lad had taken the bags up to one of the rooms without being told where to go, so this must be a usual thing. They each had their own room and that's where they entertained their guests. Now he could see why they wouldn't be overheard for at the top of the curved staircase, their room was to the left and Luce and Josh were off to the right with doors in between.

"Well at least that's something." He thought with a degree of relief while hoping the rooms were en suite as he didn't fancy parading his tackle half way across the landing trying to find a bathroom.

"Do you like it?" Zena broke into his thoughts.

"Like it? It's amazing. You never said it was like this."

A magnificent four poster bed dominated the centre of the room.

"No, it's not a bad little hole I suppose."

She went over to a door, opened it and said "All mod cons, of course it wasn't built like this but you have to have every convenience these days don't you?"

"Ah, the bathroom." He didn't know quite what else to say.

"Well let's toss our stuff on there," she indicated to a chaise longue "and get down for lunch. Well it's dinner really, then they will leave some food for later for us to help ourselves and they will all shoot off."

He refrained from saying "Oh jolly hockey sticks!" But his mind floated back to work. The lads wouldn't know how wealthy she was and what a shock it would be when he told them on Monday. Then there wouldn't be any jibes and innuendos, after all it was only jealousy because he had pulled.

Frank was getting a little apprehensive as the morning wore on. His feelings had been mixed since Joan almost forced his hand and it was because he had felt a strange leaning towards her that he had gone along with it. You didn't have to be clever to work out that she was arranging a relationship with her niece and this was playing on his mind. Especially as he had seen Evie a few times in the shop and found her to be very tasty. The problem there was the opposite. She was young enough to be his daughter and hadn't shown any feeling towards him so he'd better put that thought out of his head. Didn't anyone of his own age fancy him? Plus there was the other matter. He was still a virgin.

Cyn was now out for revenge big style. The evil was putting sadistic thoughts into her mind and her taste was turning to sado-masochism. She wanted to hurt for the sexual pleasure of it and watch others beg for mercy. With a little help from the demons it didn't take long for her to make a few contacts, starting small then hopefully building up to the heavy stuff. But that would have to be on someone else's premises, not her own. If Amy was hoping to raise her standards, it was possible that Cyn's would go the other way even to the depths of depravity but she would make sure she took someone with her.

If the demons were on full power, so were the angels. Sofia was co-ordinating the personal guardians of everyone involved even to the slightest degree. They knew they were being monitored by the evil which made it all the more difficult to stay ahead of the game. When the evil inserted it's power, the angels were equally asserting a force against them so unknown to those in body the fight going on around them was raging, with each side fighting for supremacy.

As Cyn and Amy were being coaxed away to a more exciting lucrative way of existence, their guardians nullified some of the emotion so that they still had a will of their own, but then the evil would light a new fire and goad them with rewards, which is what draws people to the bad side.

Melba and Vin were trying to calm the atmosphere around Joan and Maria but the evil force controlling Joan was gathering momentum by the minute and she could be a strong opponent. Beaty still seemed to be untouched and with resident guards seconded to her, Sofia was able to oversee what was happening first hand rather than from a distance.

Strangely enough, Dick wasn't being targeted by the hardened evil as much as the lower playful ones at this time. But this was for a reason and that would soon become clear.

Sometimes the higher powers let the underlings do all the dirty work them move in when the subject is at a low ebb or been rejected, then they just pick them off and there is no escape.

They had finished a lovely meal and retired to their rooms. The cook and any other staff would finish their duties and be gone until the next morning. Dick was still wondering what it was about Luce that he didn't feel comfortable with. She had been eying him up over dinner and the more he saw of her the more repulsed he became.

"Must have had a hard life."

He thought as he followed Zena up to the love nest.

It was becoming clear that this was a usual practice with the two women. They both acquired a lover for the weekend, brought them here and got straight on with the business, no shame, embarrassment or anything. Obviously the men of the moment just went along with it. He had to admit it certainly was different to banging away with the likes of Cyn, and it didn't seem as though he was going to have to pay for it. Surely there was a catch somewhere.

He started to get a little suspicious when they had shut the door to the room and were alone. She went to one of the mirrors on the wall and slid it to one side revealing a camera which was directed straight towards the bed.

"Oh No." He didn't expect this. "It's not one of those?"

She laughed. "By one of those you mean a voyeur cam. No, don't worry this is purely for our own enjoyment. You see when you are engrossed shall we say, you won't remember everything, well not the way I'll massage you, so when you are recovering we can watch so you don't miss anything."

"How do I know it's only you and I that will see it?" He was very uncertain.

"You have proof before you." She indicated the large screen on the wall.

"Which means what?"

"It means that I'm not showing you anyone who was here before so likewise I'm not going to show you to anyone else who may be in here in the future. Only me."

"Well."

He'd have to go along with it for now and see what happened but he would make sure he was in full control of his body functions the whole time.

"Just hope I don't fart." He thought which was quite common when he was really pumping up the action.

She had come over to the bed and pulled him down, until she was lying on top of him.

"I don't know how you usually work," she purred "but I like to give you extreme pleasure then you can do it to me."

"Oh, don't you normally, well you know I go into you and then...."

"Oh my dear man, you're going to experience a new world this weekend. It isn't just pumping off into whoever's handy you know.

It's an art. It is ultimate satisfaction, and I expect you've never ever had that."

Without realising, she had stripped him to the waist while she spoke and was now working on his belt which was off in a flash.

"Well you certainly have done this before." He didn't know why he said anything so naff and could have bitten his tongue but it was too late. Fortunately she didn't seem to have paid any attention to it so he thought he may as well lie back and enjoy the ride, so to speak. It wouldn't have mattered to her what his reaction was as long as the end product was satisfactory to her needs.

After a while he forgot the camera was there and she really was working on parts he'd never realised could make him so ecstatic. Soon he became desperate for her to finish the job as he felt he couldn't wait and it was going to take its own course if he wasn't careful. He was in agony now and begged her to let him come although it was too late but she coped with it. He lay there panting and would have to admit, this had been like nothing he'd ever had. She knew all the tricks and how to use them to perfection. The only problem was, how was he going to give her as good? There was no way he could get one up yet and he knew he didn't have the finesse to perform on her without inserting it.

It didn't seem to bother her and she was certainly in no rush so they lay there for a while. He suddenly remembered the camera.

"When do we see that?"

"Oh plenty of time. It's not complete yet."

"Eh?"

"Well there's me to go on, and then both of us together. But we've got loads of time, so no need to rush anything."

Very unromantically he said "I need to pee." Got up and made his way to the bathroom. He looked at the mirror. Did that have a camera behind it? Strangely he didn't have the kind of feelings he had expected and was becoming paranoid about the slightest thing.

His guardians were dampening down all his erotic thoughts and emotions while the evil were trying to lure him into a sordid world but the fight that was going on around him was much fiercer than any sexual act that was being filmed.

Chapter 9

Saturday afternoon was going to be very interesting for some but an eye opener for others. Joan had made sure that she and Maria were at Beaty's in good time.

"It's not tea time yet is it. Have I been asleep?" Beaty looked a bit surprised.

"No Mum." Maria gave her a kiss. "You've had your sandwich that aunt Joan left you for lunchtime." They'd checked the kitchen and the food had gone.

"Oh. I bet I nodded off again." She gave a little chuckle.

"Do you know Mum, don't say anything but I could do with one now."

Beaty patted her lap like she used to.

"Put your head on here then."

This nearly brought tears to Maria's eyes but she swallowed hard and said "I'd better not, there's a visitor coming, remember."

"Who's that then?"

Maria pretended to whisper although she knew her aunt would be listening the other side of the door.

"It's that friend of Aunt Joan's." She pointed towards the kitchen.

"Oh. Do I know her?"

"It's a him, not a her Mum."

"Oh I get it. She's got a feller." She gave a knowing look and a nod.

It was obvious she'd forgotten all about any previous mention of him but this was expected now which was why Maria was telling her as if it was the first time she'd heard it.

If Joan was listening she chose that moment to reappear. She crossed to the window and looked up and down the street.

"Weather's not too bad. Don't think we'll get that rain they forecast."

She was getting a bit anxious in case Frank didn't come after all but at that moment she saw his car slowing down as he looked for the house numbers. She was across the room in a shot and had the front door open before Beaty could even ask if a flea had bitten her, which was one of her usual retorts where Joan was concerned.

He parked and got out of the car slowly knowing she was waiting for him like a predator and once in her clutches there would be no escape.

The angels were monitoring this fully aware of the evil presence which was waiting just as eagerly for the meeting. Maria must be protected at all costs and the guard was reinforced. The angels round Joan were aware of the strength of the evil trying to eject them but they were experienced and pre-empted every move. This made the evil more determined to win the souls for themselves for they felt nothing could stop them.

"Frank!" Joan's welcome must have been heard up the street.

He gave a nervous "Hello," and followed her into the house.

As expected she made her entrance into the lounge as if she was introducing the next variety act.

"This is Frank, my colleague at work. This is my sister Beaty."

He shook hands with her.

"Hello Mrs...?

"Oh call her Beaty, she prefers it. And this... is my beautiful niece Maria."

"Hello, it's very nice to meet you." Again he shook hands, 'very limply like a bit of wet fish' were Beaty's thoughts.

"Well do sit down, make yourself at home, we don't stand on ceremony here."

Maria had been ready for this and made sure she was sitting in the other armchair opposite Mum, leaving the two seater sofa for him and Joan which wasn't exactly what her aunt had planned.

"You have him, I don't want that." Maria thought as she smiled sweetly back at the pair. The angel's power was working. There was already a block in place. So that scheme was off before it had even started.

Joan held the chairman's position from now on and the other two wondered if the poor lad would ever get chance to speak. Eventually he held up his hand to silence her.

"Mrs.. um Beaty," he turned in her direction "I can certainly advise your family as to the correct procedures so that we can get the right help for you."

"What help? I don't need help, they look after me. I don't want any strangers in here."

"I understand." He said softly. Then turning to Joan directly said "It's been lovely meeting your family. Then to Maria "I'm afraid I have another call now so I must take my leave of you."

With that he stood up, gathered his bags and shook hands with Beaty leaving Joan open mouthed.

"But….. I thought…. I mean….." She didn't know what to say. All her plans had been dashed, the angels had seen to that.

Nodding to everyone he was at the front door before another word could be uttered. Joan was after him not accepting her plan had flopped.

"But I thought you'd stay and have a meal with us."

"So sorry. I'll pop into the shop and leave the leaflets for you and you have to take it from there. I only can get involved when there is a case number you see."

She wasn't entirely sure if he was making some of this up but had no option but to let him go as he was already nearly at his car. The evil was pushing her to follow him but the angel strength held her back and returned her to the house.

Maria was relieved. She had known something was planned and even if he'd been nice she wasn't interested. Agreed, he wasn't really bad looking, that wasn't it. There was something about his general vibes that repulsed her. At first she thought it was his insipid way of speaking and moving but there was more. The angel's block had done its trick and there was no way that this relationship would even get off the ground.

Joan was torn between anger and feeling like a damp squib. She was used to organising, having people follow her ways without question, not being tossed aside. Much as she tried to hide it her mood was apparent to the others.

"Didn't like him much. Like a limp lettuce leaf."

Beaty at least brought some humour to it although that didn't help. Maria smiled and said "Don't worry, he won't be back."

Joan felt so awkward she went out into the kitchen to gather her thoughts.

"If that's the best she can do, I'd not bother." Beaty whispered to Maria.

"Me neither." She laughed quietly.

"Bit young."

"I know." Maria was about to say that a bit of matchmaking had been planned but decided against it as by now Beaty would almost have forgotten who he was and she hadn't the energy to explain.

"She sulking?" Beaty could be quite droll sometimes.

"Oh probably."

The atmosphere round these two was lightening by the second and the good spirits were cleansing the room and ousting any evil intruders who then immediately homed in on Joan. That brought even more guardians in and soon the evil realised they had to back off for a while. This house was not easy picking any more. But they would wait until she was back home because there they had a good base and the positions were reversed as that was where they were keeping as much good away as possible.

The only thing that now entered Maria's mind was how on earth was she going to survive the rest of the weekend with Joan? She decided that when they got back to her place, if her attitude hadn't changed, she would decide to go, offend or please. It was still grating that she felt she had been used, whether it be for her own good or not. She was married and didn't need any more complications. Hadn't she got enough with Dick's way of life and if he cleared off it would be a long time before she would trust a man again. No, she decided, her aunt had done more harm than good and she needed to keep her nose out of other people's business.

The angels had scored again by opening her eyes and giving her the fight to cope.

Amy was at a loose end. Her cleaning jobs were only on certain days in the week and previously Saturday had been a night when Cyn had arranged a bit of action. Here again, while the angels were trying to keep her away from that woman, the evil mischief makers were goading her to pick up the phone. Before she could decide it rang which made her jump. She didn't recognise the number and wondered whether to answer it but curiosity won and she gave in.

"Hello." The voice was very tentative.

"Amy it's me."

"Oh yes, the chap from work, you never did tell me your name."

"No. that's right. Anyway, as luck would have it something has come up next Wednesday night. Sounds good. Interested?"

"Well yes, but I work until nine o'clock."

"Sweetheart, what you earn in a week scrubbing, you could be earning in an hour."

"Oh, really, I um I don't know what to do."

His tone seemed to change at this point.

"Look, yes or no? I don't do this to mess about lady, you're either in or you're not."

"Oh yes please, sorry I can say I'm sick that night."

"Whatever, that's up to you."

He followed up by giving her instructions as to where she would be picked up and in what vehicle and told not to tell anyone or her job would be gone.

"We rely on secrecy. The clients come to us on the understanding we don't divulge anything about them so don't go prying. Your name will be Amity, understand."

"Oh. Yes alright."

"That's to protect you so don't give anybody your phone, where you live, anything about yourself. Understood?"

"Oh yes I understand. Thank you."

The call had ended.

She so wanted to get Cyn's advice on this as it felt a bit strange and a little out of her depth but she knew what would happen. Cyn would march in, take the jobs and she would be left with nothing. So if this was the start of a new opportunity she wasn't about to share it with anyone.

"He still didn't tell me his name." She thought but it didn't occur to her that this was how things were going to be from now on. Nobody's true identity would be known.

"Might as well be a number." She thought but then she remembered. "Amity. I like that. I think I'll change my name to that".

For some reason, something in her brain reminded her that was the whole point, that was how she would be known in this new world, not in her everyday life. She didn't even query how he had got her number.

Her guardians knew they had their work cut out now, especially as the evil attached to Cyn had left its mark on her. But one thing was for sure. It wasn't going to be boring.

It was as if the word had gone round to leave Cyn alone. Never had she been so quiet and she blamed Amy for it. Well something had to be done about her but first she needed hard cash. There was nothing else for it but to go down town tonight and visit a few of her previous haunts. She'd be sure to pick up some action there and as soon as she had enough cash, she'd ditch it. This would only be on a temporary basis of course but there were always talent scouts around so you never knew just what you could hook on to. Her mind was set on the big stuff but she had to work alone and not drag apprentices along with her. Not good for her image. So she would spend the afternoon dolling herself up a bit and making the goods on offer attractive.

It had been arranged between Sofia and Beaty's spirit that she take several naps so that they could be in frequent contact, and none of the earth side would query it in the least.

They were in conference with Vin discussing Maria.

"I don't want Joan brought into any discussion at the moment." Sofia stated firmly. "The evil attaching itself to her is not of the lower kind. It's hanging back in the hopes we will believe it's just a playful sprite having a bit of fun, but it is much deadlier that that. It is after possession and using her as its base."

"And Maria is with her all weekend." Vin was worried. "And she's not happy about it. Wouldn't take much to pull her out."

Beaty had been listening and said "Did you see how uncomfortable she was at my place?"

"Couldn't miss it." Vin was quick to agree but also added "The vibes when that Frank came."

"And that's another problem." Sofia came in quickly.

"Something weird about him." Beaty said. "Didn't notice it so much when I was in body but as soon as I released from it, it was very strong."

"Joan wants a match there, but Maria won't be interested in the slightest. Her body language said it all let alone her spiritual one."

Both Sofia and Vin agreed because they had both picked up a strong rejection.

"And," Beaty said what they were all aware of, "we've got to keep Maria as far away from Joan until we know what this evil thing is up to."

Vin added the fact that she was already at risk from what was hovering round her husband and that was showing signs of getting more dangerous by the minute.

"Have you seen it?" Vin asked. They all knew of Zena's attachment.

"Yes and his weekend isn't over yet." Beaty mused.

"It's what else clings to him and he brings back to our girl." Was the united agreement.

They were all in thought for a moment then Beaty said "Have we considered the fact that Joan will seek us out in spirit?"

"No doubt about it. She always did like to be in on everything but don't worry, we'll give her enough to keep her busy." Sofia and Vin both saw the funny side for they knew what could be done when needed.

"I'd better be getting back, my line is pulling." Beaty was aware of attention from her body so left quickly.

Joan was still in a huff because her plan hadn't worked to her satisfaction and the evil was jibing at her telling her it was all Maria's fault and she should do something about it.

Maria on the other hand was being pulled away by Vin in an attempt to get her back to her own place.

"I'm sorry but I really don't feel very well at the moment, and if you don't mind I'd rather be back home." Her face was quite drained but Joan had the answer.

"In which case you need looking after and you don't want to be on your own now do you? Now you just stay put and I'll look after you."

"But I….." Maria tried to get up but something was holding her in the chair.

Vin pulled with all power she could muster but couldn't lift her. This evil was stronger than she thought and it was enveloping even her.

Spirits have their own way of summoning help. A bit like the ant community. If something happens to one, the message goes through the whole colony and soon Vin had strong back up helping her outwit the opposition. Maria was almost shot from her seat her strength returning.

"Look Aunt Joan, I appreciate you are trying to help, but I really do need to be on my own for a while or I will freak out. Now please listen. I don't want to fall out with you but I've had just about as much as I can stand recently and I need my space. I feel as though I'm being stifled. I can't breathe. Now do you get it?"

With that she stormed upstairs not knowing where the energy was coming from. Joan stood open mouthed and for once at a loss for words. Then the evil pushed her anger to the fore.

"Well of all the ungrateful little bitches, after all I've tried to do for her and Beat. Well they can all get on with it." Her eyes went to the ceiling knowing Maria was collecting her things.

"You want to be on your own, then so be it. You manage your mother. You'll soon come crawling back. And you insulted my friend when I was only trying to help. I'm finished with you. Ungrateful cow."

If she expected an apology she was very disappointed for all she heard was the front door bang as Maria left, got in her car and drove back to the safety of her own house.

It was late afternoon, the two couples were in their own bedrooms for the next session. Zena suddenly suggested Dick take a breather and have a little stroll around outside.

"You'll see just what grounds we have and I've got a couple of calls to make so go and get some fresh air for a few minutes." She purred.

It wasn't so much a suggestion as an order and he knew there was no use complaining

"What's she up to?" He wondered. Being used to straightforward banging he was having to adjust to this new way of doing things.

"Must be how the rich do it." He thought, not that he was complaining but it seemed that those who had the money called the shots and you didn't argue if you wanted the pleasures.

"Wonder if they're like that among themselves."

He didn't go far, just cast an eye on the expanse of the place then slowly went in and up the stairs. As he went back into the room there was no sign of Zena.

"Are you there?" He called quietly.

"Just in the bathroom, won't be a minute darling. Why don't you get ready for me?"

"So, do I get to do it for real this time?" Dick was keen to get his end away in the fashion he was used to and while he had been in the clouds he still hankered after something he was at home with.

There was no reply so he started to undress.

The reason for her getting him out of the way to check the camera was ready for the next session, its presence he seemed to have forgotten about for now.

"I hope you'll like this." She called. "Did it specially for you."

"I hope I will, whatever it is." He muttered but was thinking "Get on with it."

The sight that met his eyes made his jaw drop to the ground.

"Oh my bleeding god!" Was all he could utter.

She looked amazing. She had on the skimpiest pair of briefs with matching bra covered in sequins. There was a sort of see though gown with things dangling from it was the only way he could describe it.

"Now you see why I asked you to leave for a moment so you could have the full on effect." She lied.

"Well, I er don't know what to say, I mean, nobody has ever ..I mean.." He was fumbling.

"It's alright, I'm used to it. Very few men can say their wives give them this kind of entertainment."

He just stopped himself replying "And that's what you are here for."

Instead he eyed her up and as she drew nearer his hand went out.

"Can't wait to see what you've got under there." He was dribbling.

"Well, now is as good a time as any."

She pushed him back onto the bed. Whatever he was anticipating was nothing like he was about to see. With a huge smile she turned her back and undid her bra and tossed it over her shoulder to him. Then she started to pull down her briefs, stopped, looked over her shoulder and said "Ready."

"You bet."

As she turned she slowly slid her panties down to show what looked like a woman's personal bits. So engrossed was he, he failed to notice that with the bra her tits had come off as well and she was flat chested. Then he looked again and got the full length view.

"But you've got no…… and you've got no um……either." He was confused.

"Does this answer your questions?"

She unhooked the sides of the briefs and whipped them off throwing them to him but at the same time put her hand down and did a bit of a wiggle and exposed her or rather his three piece suite.

"You're a……."

"Quick aren't you. Now what were you saying about doing it the right way?"

"Now you just get away from me. I don't go there. I'm straight and that's how I like it." He was grabbing his clothes and trying to cover himself as quickly as possible.

Zena was leaning over him.

"Really, that's not what you said a short while ago now is it. You weren't complaining then." Even the voice had changed.

"What have I done? You should have said. You got me here under false pretences, and that's not all that's false is it?"

"Oh dear, get a grip, this is the real world love. Accept it. Enjoy it."

"Like bloody hell I will. Now let me go home."

He smirked. "Well that's not possible you see, they" he indicated to the other room, "won't want to go yet."

"Oh, your mum, yes. Did she get you into this?"

"Ha Ha, my mum. Wake up Dick. That's not my mum."

There was a pause.

"Oh no. You're not going to tell me….. yes, I knew there was something funny about her. Hang on. She, I mean that's a bloke too isn't it?"

Zena shrugged with a sadistic smirk on her face.

"You haven't lived."

"Well I'd rather not if it's like this sordid mess, thank you. Now, I'm going home."

"Ok. How?"

"Well if you aren't going to take me I'll get a taxi."

"Oh will you? Where will you tell them to come?"

"Well here of course. I mean…."

"Exactly. Where is here?" Zena was really playing with him now. "I think the best thing you can do is sit back and enjoy the rest of your stay."

"Like hell. That's till tomorrow. I want out now or I'll blow the whistle on the filthy lot of you."

"Oh you amateurs." He sighed. "What people do on their own property is their own business and as long as they aren't annoying anybody else there is nothing anybody can do about it. Out here, who is going to complain?"

"Well just keep away from me that's all." After drawing breath he added "And I want to sleep on my own, I'm not having you dirty bastards climbing all over me. Now I see why they call you filthy rich. Well I'll stay poor working class."

She was smiling all the way through the rant then slowly got up pulled her scant clothes on and switched on the screen.

"I know it's a shock," the tone was very patronising, "but let's just watch a bit of tv shall we? I'm sure I can find something relaxing for you."

"I can do without rel……." His words trailed off as the screen sprang to life for there he was on full view being serviced by a beautiful woman, who was now smiling at him from the body of a man.

He felt sick then the truth dawned on him.

"Who sees this?"

"Oh purely for medical reasons sweetie. You know, sperm donors when they need a bit of help to toss. This always produces the goods".

He knew he didn't believe a word of it but was too shocked to say. However the next blow was about to be delivered.

"Funny how you keep bumping into people isn't it?"

"What now?" Dick hardly dare ask.

"Well, there's a mechanic at your place. Seen him before."

"Oh shit!"

"I'm sure he recognised me when I came in."

"Hang on." The light was dawning but Dick had to ask. "He knows what you are?"

"Of course."

"Christ Almighty, he'll blab to the other lads."

"By now, they'll all know I should think. Not something you keep to yourself is it?" The words couldn't have been more mocking or cutting.

There was silence while all this sank in. Then Dick looked straight at him and asked "So tell me. What are you, gay, bi? What?"

"Why do I have to be anything to fit into your little boxes? I don't go round with a tag on me."

"No, that's carefully hidden." Then Dick pointed to the screen again. "That was private. If I'd known and agreed to it, I should have been paid for it."

"Oh, now it's business is it? How quickly they turn when the pound signs light up. But there's one thing you haven't noticed."

"Oh, What's that?"

"Who said that was you?"

Dick spluttered. "Well you know it is, it's what we did a while back."

"Who says? Can't see your face."

They both studied the screen. Sure enough there was nothing to identify Dick at all and he couldn't prove it, even if he wanted to.

"I just don't believe it." He was almost talking to himself. "They thought I was having a dirty weekend. Well it doesn't get much dirtier does it? Four blokes! Four blokes." He repeated as if it would help him understand. "I'll never live it down."

How he was going to spend the next hours was now beyond him.

Dick's angels were having a job to keep his good side strong because he was now attracting all sorts of entities. This was prime entertainment and they weren't going to miss it. But the underlying evil had a stronghold and would use his current feelings for revenge and it wouldn't be pretty.

The lower levels would have their fun but soon be off to the next performance, flitting from one to the other but never really making a base. The higher level evil infiltrated a willing host then took full control so when friends would say how a person had changed, this was usually the reason. The sad part was that the person had virtually invited them by their actions. Dick would certainly be taking more home than he came with.

Maria was now enjoying her time alone. It was peaceful. Vin had calmed the whole house so wherever she went, the same feeling surrounded her. She couldn't remember when she had felt so at ease with herself, with life and even her mum. Joan was being kept out of her thoughts at the moment so that she could think logically when she had to address the situation, but for now she was unwinding beautifully.

"How's it going?" Sofia wondered.

"Really well. If only we could keep her like this." Vin was hopeful but at the same time, practical and knew that things had to be faced and dealt with. Melba had joined them not happy with the way the two women had parted and wanted a quick reconciliation.

"She needs to be separate for a while." Vin insisted.

"But it will only make it worse when they do make contact." Melba was insistent.

Beaty had also joined them and was agreeing with Vin.

"She'll snap. I don't want to see that."

Sofia knew she had to act as chairman.

"As things are reasonably quiet at the moment, let the girl have a peaceful interlude to build her back up. Don't forget she's got Dick returning tomorrow and we all know what kind of encounter that's going to be."

"I think Joan's relationship with her should be mended first and get that out of the way." Melba wasn't letting go.

"Right." The airwaves ripped as Sofia really took charge. "She has today to collect her thoughts and build her strength. Tomorrow Melba you can start to arrange a reconciliation but no arguments mind, leaving you Vin to guard her with as much back up as you need. She is vulnerable and must be protected to the hilt."

There was no question about this and everyone had an angle that suited them so they continued with their individual roles. All this had taken place while the spirits were in presence with their charges, but their souls had engaged on a higher level so at no time was a single person left unattended. One may have to witness this art to fully understand it.

Melba had been fully aware since Maria left that a touch paper had been lit. The evil wasn't even trying to hide the fact and made themselves known to any guardians that were in presence. The message was "This one is now ours." A good spirit doesn't let go however tough the opposition and help is called in to reinforce the good powers but the problem is always that the subject doesn't want it. They need to go ahead with revenge, spite, anything they feel is their due so they are in fact working against their angels but that is how the evil plan it.

Beaty had woken up in her chair.

"What time of day is it?" She said aloud then followed on with "What day is it?"

As there was no reply she must be alone. What was happening? It was ages since she'd seen anyone.

"They must all be at work." Was her first thought.

She sat for a while wondering what to do. It seemed to her she should have a wash but that was a bit hazy. Something to eat? Not really hungry.

Then she thought she should go to the toilet but that made her realise she felt rather wet down below. This started to distress her and within minutes she was softly sobbing. It didn't occur to her to do anything about it, the logic had gone.

"I didn't think it'd come to this." She whispered.

Never in her life had she felt so alone, so unwanted and unimportant. People had their busy lives and there wasn't time for her. This was how she felt for she didn't realise it was only yesterday when three people had been sitting there and someone would be in to see to her shortly. It was like the computer that hadn't saved the recent information.

Sofia sent her into a short sleep to release her for a moment.

"Oh I hate that." Beaty looked at her body. "How much longer?"

Sofia had to be honest.

"A while yet. Your body isn't ready to give up, even if your mind is."

"It's cruel. Not only for me, but anyone like it and the family must be going through hell watching and can't do anything about it."

"You know we see it from both sides all the time."

Beaty was quiet for a moment then stated the obvious. "But it's different when its one of yours, or even you."

Sofia knew very well.

"Would it help if you didn't make so many release moments. Do you want to stay awake longer?"

"Not really. There's work to do and at least I feel useful if we have a job on."

"Which you won't remember when you wake up." Sofia sent a wave of humour through the thought.

"Might think I'd been dreaming though."

With that she returned to being the sad lady waiting for company.

Chapter 10

There was a dilemma. Joan wouldn't ignore her sister but didn't want to ask Maria if she was going. It was Sunday morning so neither of them would be at work. Maybe she would just pop round then if madam turned up so be it. At least Beaty would be looked after and she would make sure there was no argument in front of her. She was still seething inside as she liked to be top dog and someone had actually gone back at her. But forget that. Beaty's needs came first.

Maria likewise was wondering what to do. Her love for her Mum was stronger than anything her aunt threw at her so she decided she would go round without asking Joan what she was doing. If they both turned up, she would be polite but keep the visit short. She was feeling quite refreshed and decided that it would be best if her husband went away a lot more. Oh he'd still live there but not be there too much. That would be perfect. New decision, new start.

The angels were observing these plans and were ready in the wings to make sure everything stayed calm.

Cyn had had a rough night. Yes she'd earned a bit but at what cost? Dropping her standards for a while had attracted the sort she'd long ditched and now she was back. The word would soon go round and her upper class customers wouldn't touch her with a yard stick.

"It's all that cow's fault. She did this." She fumed as she reached for a cigarette. Amy was on her hit list now and she would pay.

"After all I done for her."

Here was another one out for revenge but big time and if she had her way the woman would never work again. She may never even walk again. Cyn was going through a list of contacts in her mind, those that weren't banged up at the moment, but there were those that never got caught. Trouble was they demanded more funds and they weren't available just now. Well, the old trick would have to come into play. You scratch mine etc.

The subject of her revenge was looking forward to Wednesday, at least she thought she was. It was strange going on her own to a place she didn't know where it was, and with people she'd never met. But she wouldn't know if she didn't give it a try and if it was no good she needn't go again. Or so she believed. There was no one to advise her now of how these things worked, and more to the point who you were working for, although you could class yourself as self employed rather than unemployed if you wanted to impress. But it was all just words really, it didn't alter what you were.

"What do I wear?" Amy was going through her few clothes. She could really do with a complete overhaul but couldn't afford it right now.

"I know," she had an inspiration "when I do the morning job I'll go in the charity shops. Pick up a few bits there."

She was thinking along the lines of skimpy skirts, tight tops even some fashion boots if they were cheap enough and that would have to do. She certainly would look to see what the others were wearing and then get something with her earnings. After all, this was work and she had to look right.

He didn't know how but Dick had managed to get some sleep. This had to be a nightmare, it couldn't be real, but as his senses returned and he looked round the room he knew only too well it hadn't been a dream. He was alone. This made him a bit insecure. The thought hit him that they had all cleared off and left him there, wherever it was.

Although he was in no hurry to face any of them, it couldn't be put off so he had a quick shower and shave and got dressed. For some reason he was very hungry now so slowly made his way down stairs towards the kitchen.

"Breakfast is in there." The voice made him swing round to face the voice. He had to look again. It had to be Luce but not in all the trimmings she, correction he was wearing yesterday. He was also eying Dick up with some appreciation which immediately unnerved him again.

"Oh thank you." He rushed past him and into the dining room. "I've got to get out of here or I'll go mad." He was muttering as he came face to face with Zena and Josh.

"Morning."

They both chorused then Zena asked "Sleep well precious?"

Dick turned his back to get some cereal and gave a very indistinct "Yes."

"Oh good. Ready for the next then."

He spun round now.

"Let's get one thing straight."

At that word the other two hooted with laughter as Luce joined them.

Dick was getting more angry than anything now as his demons were goading him into conflict.

"I am not into your kind of stuff. Not now, not never. You do what you want, it's of no concern to me. But leave me bloody well out of it." He was shouting the last bit.

Zena, in her full female attire had stuck the edge of her bottom on the corner of the table where he was about to sit.

"No, you listen dearie. You don't think you came here for a free ride do you? Oh no. You take the pleasure, but you pay."

"Like hell. You're getting nothing out of me." He was livid.

There was a snigger among the others as Zena said "I think I already have if you think about it."

"You're disgusting."

"Ho, listen to Mr self righteous. No sweetheart, you take, you give."

"I repeat you're….."

"Shut up and listen." She was in his face now. "You don't do half a job, you finish it."

The other two had closed in. He felt claustrophobic.

Luce joined in now.

"It's nothing for a man of your qualifications, you can easily complete what you started. And it was very good I understand."

"What are you talking about?" All of a sudden his hunger had gone.

The others took it in turn to explain.

"Nice little start to the film."

"Middle quite tasty too."
"Can't wait to see the last part."
He pulled away from them.
"Now if you're talking about that piece of garbage you showed me, you don't need me. Anyone could have finished that off."
Then looking round them all said very slowly "Any one of you."
It went quiet for a moment then Josh spoke.
"Just depends on whether you want to walk out of here."
For the first time utter terror took over. They were all closing in and were blocking him from going anywhere.
"You can't do a thing. I am a free man." The panic sounded in his voice.
"Have a cup of tea and we will explain."
"There's nothing to explain. I'm going. Sorry but that's it."
There was silence as the tea was pushed towards him. He took a couple of sips to give him time to regroup and come up with something. Then he laughed.
"I've just realised. You can't film me doing ..well that, I mean where would I put it?"
As soon as the words left his mouth he realised what he'd said. He'd been thinking of straight sex but there was no woman here so the kind of film wouldn't be what he had first thought.
"Would you like us to provide you with one?" Luce was swinging a spoon from her fingers as though she was hypnotising him.
He thought for a moment. If he wanted to get out of here unscathed, could that be the answer? Especially if his head was out of shot.
"Well, at least it would be normal, for me that is." But then he said "Who? There's only us here isn't there?"
"Oh dear, you really don't pay attention do you?" Zena was being very smug. "There's a few others remember, day staff."
"Oh them. Yes."
"Well?" Luce was still swinging her spoon.
"OK. But you promise it will be female."
"You have my word." Josh confirmed.
It was hard to say who breathed the biggest sign of relief, Dick or the rest of them but for different reasons.

Frank had gone home after the family encounter. He knew before he went that Joan had more than the welfare of her sister at heart and now he saw her in a different light. She looked old, hard and very calculating and he would limit his visits to the charity shop when she wasn't likely to be there. Maria was quite tasty but too much baggage to cope with. He liked them free and as unattached as possible to keep life simple. His mind turned to Evie. Very nice but would she suit his taste? Bit too young and not as worldly as she would have anyone believe. Also she would have friends but they would be like her so that was another closed door. So he would have to keep searching for now because somewhere out there would be just what he was seeking.

The angels were now on full alert. Joan's caring side was turning to one of torment, bullying and enjoying seeing the weak ones suffer at her expense. Sofia feared for Beaty who agreed with the fact that she was safe in spirit but as soon as she had to return to her body she would be at the hands of a monster. They would have to find a way for Maria to take over her care, or, and this wasn't a pleasant option, Beaty would have to be placed in a care home.

"But how safe will she be there?" Melba was more than aware of the change in Joan but knew of the kind of things that went on behind closed doors in some homes. If it was a good one, it would be alright but how could they be certain?

"We'll have to do the homework from here." Beaty had joined them and picked up on the problem. "What's wrong with vetting them from spirit and then picking the best."

"Perfect." Sofia agreed, then came the 'but' word. "But what is the betting they will have no room?"

Melba came out with a very strong statement.

"Unless we make room."

There was stillness for a moment. This option had been used in the past but only when someone was so close to transition that a few hours wouldn't make any difference and would be looked on as a blessing.

"Sounds awful I know," Beaty offered "but there is another path to follow."

Sofia knew what was coming. "You'd take yourself over now."

Nobody had to comment as there was the main factor to consider. If Beaty died, to put it in plain speech, for one thing Joan would still seek her out in spirit, and the evil pushing Joan would simply find another target for its sadistic satisfaction in bodily form, or push Joan further to hunt out Beaty so whatever form she was using at the time would make no difference.

"Seems like we'll have to let nature take its course for now" Sofia suggested, "but the monitoring must be done by experienced angels, no lower levels."

As this seemed the only sensible course of action, Beaty returned to her body to await the onslaught from her own sister.

Vin was shadowing Maria's every move but with a small back up kept at a safe distance. They were now trailing the car as she headed towards her Mum's. She was relieved to see that Joan's car wasn't there and hoped her aunt would keep out of her way.

"It's me Mum." She called as she entered the hall.

"Hello dear." Beaty called from the lounge. "I'm in here."

"That's a relief." Maria whispered under her breath.

As she entered the room she was pleasantly surprised to see how bright Mum looked this morning.

"Did you have a good sleep?" She popped a kiss on her forehead.

"Do you know, I think I did." Beaty beamed then laughed "Do you think the witch put something in my tea?"

"Mum. You naughty lady. Hey, if she did, we'll put double in hers."

They both shared a lovely moment when Beaty seemed to be her old self but Maria knew it wouldn't last, however she would enjoy this and hopefully many more like it.

"What day is it?"

"Sunday Mum."

"Oh. They're all the same really aren't they?"

"Pretty much."

Beaty's hand went out as her daughter passed the chair.

"I love it when you come to see me."

"And I love coming Mum."

The moment brought the sting of tears at the back of Maria's eyes but she forced them back and gave her a hug.

"Do you fancy a full English, as it's Sunday, you know a small one."

"That'd be nice. Are you having some?"

Maria stopped by the door.

"Do you know, I think I will."

"Oh lovely. Then you can tell me all your juicy bits."

"Mum, I don't have juicy bits. But I bet you've had a few in your time."

"Well there were one or two but there was this one chap...."

"Mum should I be hearing this?" Maria laughed and it wasn't forced, it was so natural she wished this moment could last.

The angels were covering the place in warmth and love and it was working, not only to make the women feel better but it acted as a protective shield which was about to be proved. The evil that was trying to get into them both was being repelled as the force of love was too strong for them.

Unbeknown to them, Joan had decided to go round, lay the law down and say how things were going to be from now on. As she turned into the street she saw Maria's car parked outside the house.

"Oh yes well she'd have to get in first and put her side forward. I'll be everything that's evil now. Well, I'll put a stop to that."

But she wasn't expecting what came next. As she pulled up to the house, the wheel was wrenched from her grasp and she could only watch in horror as her car was steered round Maria's and send straight down the road. Try as she might, nothing she did make the slightest bit of difference.

"What the bloody hell?" She was screaming in terror as she tried to regain control and it was only when the car stopped abruptly at the junction did she realise the power had released her.

Nothing would have induced her to go back and she went home as fast as possible.

"I'm never stepping foot in there again." She yelled to herself as she went into her house. "She's possessed it. She is everything that is evil."

The words were being fed into her conscious mind by the evil pushing her to do something drastic. It was making her angry at the others but plotting the most horrible end to it all. And she would be doing it. Her rage was directed at Maria, but her sister was becoming a major pain and was stopping her having the life she should be enjoying, so the two of them needed removing and quickly. How she did it, didn't matter for she knew she would come up with the answer soon, but of course none of it would come back on her. She was the loving relative and would be absolutely devastated.

The day went on pretty smoothly for most people. Beaty slept for a greater part of it and Maria, between visits to her during the day went home and relaxed as she hadn't for a long time. She could cope with Mum but not him and the choice if she had to make it was a simple one. She now wanted him out of her life. How she would manage, she would have to sort out but anything would be better than living with this because he didn't seem to think he was doing anything wrong.

Although Joan seemed to have withdrawn from the scene, she was plotting her next move and then they would take notice. Of what she hadn't quite worked out yet but she would. Such was the state of her mind which was growing more sinister by the minute.

Cyn was toying with the idea of going on the town again but still feeling disgruntled at the low life which was all that seemed available but she blamed Amy for that and was seeking her own revenge, so the air was becoming like a storm cloud that was brewing but still building up for its climax.

Amy on the other hand was on the way up or so she thought. In fact she didn't really know what she felt and was in need of guidance but she would see this one through and if it was ok she only had herself to thank. It didn't sink in to her that someone else had targeted her as a worker and without them she wouldn't have had this opportunity. The evil lurkers knew they could mould her any way they wanted and she'd never realise.

Despite his previous misgivings, Frank was thinking about giving Evie a closer look. Maybe age wouldn't matter although he didn't normally go for them that young. He needed to know more about her before making a move and then it would be very calculated. He never did anything on the spur of the moment. Every manoeuvre was carefully thought through and only when he was sure did he put anything into action.

Surprisingly enough, the weekend hadn't been a total disaster for Dick who was now quite enjoying himself. He'd worked his way through two maids and now was getting ready to give the cook a sample hoping he could still deliver the goods after a short rest. Funnily enough he'd forgotten all about the cameras. Once he had been assured that his head was out of shot, he relaxed and got on with whatever he was told to do which was more a case of where to face and what angle to be using. Not the actual act he was glad to note.

After the first lass, he had even asked if he could have a viewing and by the time he'd serviced the second he needed it, not only for the short break but something to get him up and running for the cook who was about the same age as the maids, so there was not a problem there.

He was having a refreshing shower when she came in unannounced and got into the shower with him.

"Is this extra to the work?" He joked.

"I just like to be familiar with what you've got and what you do with it." Her hand was already on his pump action and it suddenly occurred to him that if he lost it here, he wouldn't be able to supply when the time came. He didn't get a chance to refuse because this one was really getting his juices flowing and without having to think of whether his cock was on full camera view they did it standing there with water running all over them. He was gasping and almost propped against the wall when she left quickly.

"Brilliant. We must have another like that."

The sounds of people coming into the bathroom made him reach for a towel.

"Ha ha too late. Got it all every last drop."

"What?" He couldn't believe it. "But there's no cameras......" He stopped as the truth dawned and looked round.

"Relax you won't see them. That's the idea." One of the men said.

"And you are?" He asked.

140

"Crew. Who else were you expecting?"
"But I thought....."
"That there was one camera in your room. I know. Understandable."

Dick had wrapped a towel round his lower region.

"So are you trying to say that the whole place is rigged?"
"Well not quite everywhere, but quite a bit of it." Was the reply.
"Am I even safe to take a crap?"

They all shrugged and left.

As he made his way to the toilet he paused for a moment and looked round the fittings. Nothing on view.

"Oh bollocks!" He said aloud "I need a piss and if anyone needs to see that good luck to them."

He was a bit hesitant to go back to the bedroom but he didn't have time to wonder for long as he was almost dragged downstairs and out onto the spacious lawns which hadn't been mowed for a while.

"Ok get on with it. Time's money." The order was far from friendly.

Zena was standing next to him now.

"Big name in this sort of thing darling, we're so lucky to have him. Don't let us down, but of course you won't."

With that she gave him a push and as another hand held onto his gown, he ended up running stark naked across the grass but he wasn't alone. The three young females were now joining him from different directions and as they pulled him down he prayed he could perform satisfactorily although that was very unlikely. The chill had given him a droop for one thing but the camera was way back so this was obviously a distance shot.

"Perhaps they won't notice." He thought.
"Fake it." One was caressing his ear with her tongue.
"Won't they know?"
"Not if you can act."
"But I thought only women....."

Before he could finish she'd given him a slap across the thigh just missing his equipment.

They seemed to be getting in some sort of formation and he wasn't sure what to do.

"Lay back and pretend to scream." One said quietly. "The sound isn't on with this one."

As he did so he noticed they were all carrying something behind their backs, the camera facing them straight on. The cook had got a large kitchen knife and was now standing over him wielding it in the air while the others were cheering her on but were close together on their knees.

"What the hell is......?" He tried to say.

"Shhh. Just look as though you're in agony when we tell you."

He soon found out what this cheap movie was going to portray. Talk about amateur!

As 'cook' brought the knife down between his legs, one had a container of a red substance which shot into the air, while the other produced a false penis, also covered in red stuff which she ran around waving in the air. He was supposed to lie there as though his willy was being paraded round the lawn. Oh this was sick and tacky.

As soon as they were told it was a wrap, they all just got up and wandered back into the house as though they'd been on a family picnic.

If he was embarrassed about what the lads would say about Zena being a bloke, thank god they would never find out about this fiasco and the sooner he was out of it the better.

"Never, never again." He was muttering as he tried to get to the house with as few seeing his floppy bits as possible.

In the bedroom Zena came in to see if he was okay. Gone was the provocative outfit and there stood a man in cropped jeans and a tee shirt.

"Alright." Dick exploded. "What do you call that load of shite? Talk about back street videos. You lot with all your money have to stoop to this."

He let him rant until his breath ran out and said very slowly "And just where do you think the money comes from to pay for a place like this? They hire it, and it's cheaper than having proper actors. So we help them and in turn it helps us."

If there was one thing certain in Dick's mind it was that he'd never fall for such a low trick again and he felt an utter fool now.

"When can I go?" He asked without looking at him.

"As soon as these bods have done. They've got to load up and everything."

"Well that won't take them long will it?"

He was quiet for a moment then asked "Just who looks at this kind of rubbish?"

"Oh come on. Don't tell me you've never watched a video or those channels that show the foreign stuff. And don't forget this has got to be edited and well, tweaked a bit."

"Tweaked?"

"Oh yes, lot of it ends up on the proverbial."

He wasn't sure what he meant.

Zena sighed. "The cutting room floor of course. You don't think they run it without checking it do you?"

"And I won't be recognised?"

Zena's mood had changed. from the sexy female pulling the prey to a very tetchy man.

"Once and for all no. Now for Christ's sake don't ask me again. Are you ready?"

"More than you know."

"Come on then I'll take you back?"

He stopped. "Aren't Luce and……..."

He chopped him off. "They'll go later now stop asking questions."

He wanted to say they if he and Zena were going in the car, but then thought that either he would be coming back or they had another in one of the out buildings. Anyway it wasn't any concern of his and he just wanted out.

"Pity I didn't get paid for my services." He couldn't help remarking as they drove along.

"You've been fed and watered and had enjoyable sex all weekend. Don't be frigging greedy."

The rest of the journey was in silence until he asked him to drop him at the garage instead of the park. He got out and they barely said farewell, both relieved to be finished but he couldn't help asking "What is your name? I mean your real name?"

As the other man revved up to pull away he said "Zena of course."

Maria had finished washing up after having had tea with Beaty and was almost dreading going home. The sound of the front door made her jump then realised it could only be Joan.

"A bit late." She thought as she wiped down the working surface. "Bet she hasn't brought her anything."

Neither of them had seen or heard from her all day and if it hadn't been for Maria, Beaty would have been left until now.

"Oh you've had your tea. Good. Thought you might have." Joan breezed into the lounge without even calling a 'good evening' to her niece.

"Just as well." Beaty didn't even turn and look at her.

Joan stopped for a moment.

"What are you saying?"

"Well I could be dead for all you'd care." Followed by a loud sniff.

"Hasn't anyone been then?" She still didn't call Maria by name or acknowledge the fact she was there.

"Good job they did or I'd have been in a sorry state."

"Well there were no arrangements made, I mean how can you sort anything if nobody is speaking to you?"

"So you'd just have left me?" Beaty's words were quiet but spoken with great sadness.

"Oh now you're being dramatic."

Joan hadn't sat down and was pacing like a dog wanting to be let out. As no answer was going to be forthcoming she moved back to the door until she was behind her sister.

"I should get a room freshener, you could cut this air with a knife. Talk about an atmosphere. Ha."

"Was alright till you came in." Beaty's whisper could just be heard.

"Well I certainly know when I'm not wanted."

She moved back until she was facing Beaty and looking down on her.

"Do not expect any help from me. It's up to you pair now. You sort it. I'm finished."

As she flounced out Beaty's voice followed her.

"Ha. Didn't come across did he?"

The slamming of the front door said more than any words could ever have done.

Maria came into the room in tears and flopped on the floor at the side of her mum.

"I'm so sorry." She sobbed as though her heart would break. "I'll look after you mum."

Beaty's hand rested on her head and her mind went back to when this was her little girl who had just had her favourite doll smashed.

"Don't you worry. We don't need her. Good riddance."

"But she was so nasty. I heard but daren't come in or I'd have gone for her. Then that would have upset you."

"I'd have cheered you on." Beaty smiled at the thought.

They sat like that for a while then the ultimate question came.

"What's the enemy say?"

"It's about half past six mum."

"Oh. What day is it?"

Maria smiled. For a brief moment she'd had her mum back when she needed her but now she had returned to her lonely lost world.

"Sunday." Maria's voice dropped as she knew the peace was about to end as Dick could be home when she got back. Or was it?

"Mum."

"Yes. What is it?"

"I've had a thought."

"Now you be careful." Beaty always said this for a laugh.

Her daughter took a deep breath.

"Well, you know I've been a bit, no, a lot pissed off with Dick just lately?"

"Oh about him running round with other women."

"How did you know about that?" She was amazed at the reply.

"Somebody told me, now who was it?"

"Well there's only one person besides me been coming round so that doesn't take a lot of working out."

"Doesn't it?" Beaty was a bit lost.

"Your precious sister."

"Joan? Oh I don't think so, wait a minute, yes it may have been now I come to think of it. Yes. There was something about you cutting his tail off."

"I see." Maria was seething. "And by the way I didn't cut it off although I came pretty damned well near it I can tell you."

"I would have."

"What?"

"I'd have had the knife ready for when the beggar came through the front door."

This lightened the mood somewhat for even if it wasn't true it was another little chink of sense that would be gone as soon as it came.

"Well, if I'm going to look after you all the time...."

"Why don't you move in here?" Beaty thought she had fallen on the idea herself.

"Well I could. I mean I've put a lot into that house and I couldn't manage if he left which is the only reason I let the creep back in."

"But this is yours when I'm gone dear. I know you're having to do a lot for me and I wish you didn't have to but at least you'd be away from him."

They both sat for a while, Maria going through the practical aspects and Beaty floating away in her world again. For a few seconds she dropped off and Sofia was ready for her.

"Great. Let her go with it. We must keep Joan away, she has a bad attachment and it mustn't get a hold here. We will guide Maria as to where to get the necessary physical help, and she will be channelled into making sure everything is legally settled."

With that Beaty woke up wondering where she was and having no knowledge of the exchange with her guardian who was still with her as always.

Joan got home feeling she had told them just how it was from now on.

"They'll see." She said out loud as she made a cup of tea. "They'll want me before I want them. I'll give it a couple days and then they will be begging for my help."

The evil had got her in this frame of mind which was leading up to utter revenge, for what? It didn't matter to start with as long as the urge was planted then she would find anything to be her reason for retaliating. Everyone would be wrong and against her and she would fight back until all she had to fight was herself. Then they would have her, along with millions of others going the same way. This was how they built up their strength, by planting the seeds and watching them grow as they were nurtured. People often wondered why a friend or relative had suddenly had a complete change of character. If they only knew that this was the reason.

Her next target would be Frank. He had been a complete and utter wash out.

"Calls himself a man! A flea has got more life in it."

She would never realise that the hint of attraction had also been planted in her to then make her feel rejected and unwanted, leading to anger and determination to get back at him in some way.

As soon as he even put his nose in the charity shop she would give him a piece of her mind and it wouldn't matter if there were customers or not, let everyone see how shallow and fake he was.

"Do gooder indeed. Fat lot of help he was to us. Like a wet fish."

She was muttering to herself as she made a sandwich. Her mind went to everyone she knew and she found fault with them all but those closest to her were going to soon feel the brunt of her anger. She wouldn't rest until they knew she wasn't one to mess with.

Melba had seen what was going on, being only too familiar with this tactic, and called in extra guard to protect her but by now this kind of evil was growing at such a pace, it was a job to keep up with it. All they could do was be diligent and inject as much positivity into her soul as they could. With every decision she would make, they would insert the element of doubt. "Why am I doing this? Isn't this wrong? Is this what I really want?"

If anyone should be questioning their way of life it should be Cyn. It was noticeable how she was lowering her lifestyle but this was how the evil was infiltrating her. It was dragging her down to the lowest level until even her self respect had gone. But she was now associating with people that would think nothing of taking her out of the picture if she crossed them. She was relying on drink and drugs to keep her going and most of the time didn't even make it home, if she even knew where that was any more. All this had happened so quickly but it takes much longer to build back to where you were, if ever. Unfortunately, this had been her way of life before she became as she thought 'respectible'. She now had a nice little house in a pleasant area but that was already under threat as the neighbours were determined to have her out of there. Nobody wanted a brothel on their doorstep so her card was already marked. It was rented so the landlord had been informed that he had better send her packing, only it wasn't put as politely as that.

Attention was also turning to Amy for the same reason and after the last little episode they were watching her very closely. At the moment all seemed quiet as she wasn't having customers to her place, and there weren't car doors being banged into the night, but they were all waiting for her to put a foot wrong. Some blamed her association with Cyn and in all fairness were prepared to see that if she could detach herself from her and lead a respectable life, they would go along with it, as long as she didn't drift back. They had their code of conduct and were determined to uphold it.

Chapter 11

Dick drove the short distance home with mixed feelings. His weekend had been a disaster to put it mildly and he wanted to forget it, but what kind of mood would his wife be in? He was sure she hadn't fallen for his excuse but he'd got to ride it out now.

"Here I am." He called as let himself in the front door.

"Come in here." It was an order.

Dropping his bag in the hallway he slowly went into the kitchen. The door was open and he could see Maria leaning on the sink both hands behind her.

"Um, did you want me?" He thought he'd better say something but wasn't quite sure what.

Her right hand came into view holding her large knife.

"No Dick. I don't want you, not in any way, shape or form. I don't want you to come anywhere near me or I will use this I promise you."

She was now waving the blade in front of him.

"Look sweetheart...."

"Don't ever call me that or any other fancy name you give your tarts."

"Look let's sit down and talk." The knife was really making him very uncomfortable.

"Oo, I don't think there's anything to talk about do you. I mean, I don't want an account of all you've been doing for the last two days, and you certainly won't want to tell me, will you now?"

"But I told you....."

"No Dick, all you told me was your usual pack of lies."

"I took Phil......"

"Shut up. You didn't and you know it and I know it."

He was about to ask how she knew but he didn't get chance.

"You really should check out your alibi if you are going to play those sort of games. You didn't take Phil or your car would have been at his place but it wasn't was it?"

"I...I.."

"And shall I tell you how I know? Because it was parked where you left it. Behind the garage. And how do I know that?"

"Obviously because you went snooping about behind my back."

Her laugh hit him

""Ha ha ha. Behind your back. That's choice. What the hell have you been doing?"

"So if you didn't see it, some nosey sod has told you."

She laughed again. "So you don't deny it."

He realised he was being backed into a corner.

"Don't suppose you are going to say because nobody has told you. You're just clutching at straws."

Her venom was rising and she didn't care how many she dragged down.

"Oh, it was Aunt Joan if you must know."

"What that interfering vicious cow. And of course you believed her."

"Why shouldn't I?"

He'd had enough. What with the events he'd just left and now this interrogation, he wasn't standing for it.

"If you've got something to say, out with it or let me go and have a shower and a beer."

"Right! Now I've got your full attention. You are on your own. You can shag who you like, you can catch whatever you like because it's now nothing to do with me. You haven't even noticed how I haven't been coping. What with you and mum's condition, I have had enough and something has to go."

"Are you putting her in a home then?"

"No!" She screamed "I'm not putting her anywhere, she's staying where she is for as long as possible."

"So what's the problem?"

"I am going to look after her."

"So what's all the fuss about, you do now."

She had been building up for this.

"Yes, but in her home. I am going to live with her. I will stay at work for as long as possible but then I may have to care for her round the clock."

He hadn't expected this.

"What? But you can't. What about me?"

"Selfish to the core, What about you? You can do what you've been doing. And I hope you enjoy it."

He was stunned, his face a picture of complete shock as she continued

"Oh yes, you are still obliged to support me so we will settle an amount for you to pay weekly or monthly, either way is fine."

"If you think...."

"Any more questions just refer them to our solicitor. I'm off now. Good bye. I will expect to be informed of the amount and frequency of the payments."

She had rehearsed the wording so that it sounded as though she had already taken steps and he didn't catch on to the fact that it was Sunday and no body would be working. Her 'get out' if he had queried it was that she had already put it in the pipe line but not said anything.

"Well done girl." Vin was jubilant and Sofia knew instantly.

With a small case already in her car, Maria left the house with mixed feelings but knew this was the path she had to take for her own sanity.

Beaty had taken a quick nap and was up to date on what Maria had done.

"At least we've got her out of his clutches. He has lost his control, but wait for the retaliation."

"We're ready for that but this, on top of his recent experience is going to knock him to a low." Sofia was summing up but then added the inevitable. "Which is when they will take complete control of him."

Beaty agreed but was also looking at it from the good side.

"His guardians must have been having a tough time but if they can get him back now before the evil really takes root, there's some hope."

"Never ending battle." Sofia was confirming the continual struggle.

"I'd better get back before she gets to my place." And Beaty was gone.

Zena, having taken Dick home had returned to the manor house as he expected but if he thought it would be to take them home he was completely wrong. They were going through the footage of the weekend's work.

"Not bad." Josh said as Zena joined them. "There's plenty we can use in several different scenes. You did well. Look at this, here he appears to be partly dressed which we can use in the Loretta clip, and here he's totally starkers so that will be in the Mandy one. And there's plenty for when I do the compilation. Customers like those."

Luce beamed at him.

"Get much off his cards?"

"Oh I did a bit of on line shopping while he was asleep. Small bits so he probably won't notice, and even if he does, he's not about to broadcast it."

"Not a bad picking then." Josh looked pleased.

"Don't forget we've got to get ready for the next ones." Luce reminded them.

"Most of it's done." Josh shut down the computer and they all settled down for a bottle or two which was their usual habit after such hard work. To see them sprawled out relaxing, they bore no resemblance to their previous appearance.

Monday had begun with people adjusting to severe changes in their lives. Apart from Beaty and Maria's arrangement, Dick had not only got to face his life alone which was a big enough shock in itself, but the thought of facing his workmates seemed just as daunting.

He couldn't see that he had done anything wrong but it would appear to him that everyone was against him and had treated him badly. And Maria had called him selfish. That he couldn't understand so put it down to someone having poisoned her mind against him and it didn't take much working out who that was.

Joan on the other hand felt she was in total control now. In her opinion she had been used, and by her own family.

"I'll show them."

She was making breakfast and laughed as she thought of how her niece would have to be rushing around getting to Beaty to see to her before shooting off to work, then back there at dinner time and goodness knows how she'd cope with the evening. Instead of any sign of remorse, she was actually thriving on it and would sit back and wait for them to come begging for her help which they would and it wouldn't be too long before that happened. But it wasn't going to stop there. The evil influence wasn't going to sit and wait, it was already controlling her mind. So not only would she be holding back from assisting, she would be stirring it up and causing more distress and unpleasantness. And she was going to enjoy every moment of it.

Melba was fighting hard to overcome this and get Joan back on track and into her own mind control but this evil cell was proving a tough opponent. Every time she tried to veer her charge away from their power, it increased against her and even with the strong back up it was becoming too much.

"Why are they using such a strong force?" She was asking Sofia.

"Does seem over the top. Could just be a distraction to get our attention from what is really going on or…" She paused.

Melba added "They are simply using her and probably many more to plant some terrible threat or the seeds of terrorism."

"That has been my worry for some time. We've seen it start so small that it went unnoticed until it was too late." Sofia wasn't giving up. "We must do a scan. Take a pattern of Joan's aura and circulate it all over the area."

"Done." It only took a milli second for Melba to spread it then added "It does follow the route of planting the contact in someone that people would least suspect. Good people, not bad."

"Which is how they slip under the radar." Sofia added.

Maria did her best to look as normal as possible when she got to work but one of her fellow office workers had been watching her. When she got a moment she asked "You ok love?"

"Yeah yeah, just a bit tired, you know how it is."

"Hmm. If you say so. You can tell me you know, I won't blab."

"I'm Ok."

The tone was saying 'enough' so the other woman backed off but she knew all was not right and wanted to get some answers, but that would have to wait for now.

It couldn't be put off any longer. Dick drove to work and parked in his usual spot. As he crossed the yard he could here faint tones of a song wafting towards him. He recognised it as 'She's a lady' and knew he was in for a rough ride. The cheer that went up when he entered the workshop said it all. Various dubious comments were hurled about but he went to his locker and ignored them apart from raising one hand in acknowledgment.

Phil had come out of the office and knew that this could go on for ever if he didn't bring some order to it.

"Alright, alright you've had your fun now can we get some work done please? Dick you've got a service coming in any time now." He called.

"You bet he has." Was a retort.

"Hope he's got the strength for it."

"Is the customer male or female?"

"Won't make any difference to him."

Phil shouted now.

"I said that's enough. Now I want to hear no more of it, not while you're at work." His expression wasn't pleasant but Dick was grateful in a small way to have the lid put on it.

The rest of the day didn't go without continual jibes but Dick had more on his mind now and so he shut off from the lads' banter and tried to work out what was going to happen regarding his home life.

There was great activity round Cyn's home. Police were there and the whole neighbourhood wondered what she had attracted now. Much as anyone tried to find out what had gone on, nothing was being divulged. As Amy came out of her front door to go to work, she asked one of the onlookers.

"I'd have thought you'd have had more idea than us."

She ignored the unkind words and much as she was dying to know she thought she would find out later anyway so left as quickly as she could. In one way it bothered her as Cyn had been good to her in some ways, but if anything unsavoury had happened she felt a slight relief that she hadn't been part of it. She'd often wondered what the woman had stashed away in the house and thought maybe they were raiding it for stolen property. And there were the naughty magazines so it might be that kind of raid. Amy wasn't sure if that was a valid reason but it could be.

She was just starting work when her mind caught up, which often took a long time.

"Oh dear. What if something's happened to her?" At last, the light came on. Perhaps she should have stayed to find out, but then she might have been questioned and that was the last thing she wanted right now.

"No, I'm better off here." She told herself, but at the same time knew she had to go home at lunch time. Something was telling her things weren't right but she couldn't work out what. The idea even crossed her mind to ring her mum but they didn't get on so it had to be an emergency before she'd do that.

Joan was on her own at the charity shop which gave her ample time to put her sadistic plan into action and she could use the phone there without interruption as it was very quiet at the moment. Firstly she rang the department that Frank worked for and asked for his superior.

"Oh hello, you won't know me but I'm afraid I have to report something." Was how she started but went on to report that Frank had been to her sister's house over the weekend and had been very discourteous. Also an item of jewellery was missing and they only noticed it after he had gone. She went on to say how upset her sister was at losing it because it had belonged to their mother. As nobody else had been in the house, it could only have been him that could have taken it.

"Could she possibly have dropped it? Have you searched everywhere?" The man on the phone asked.

"Well of course we looked. That was the first thing we did. And he wasn't kind to my sister so he shouldn't be doing that job. She was extremely upset."

The man pointed out that this was a serious allegation and would have to be looked into thoroughly so they would send someone round to speak to her but of course the police would have to be involved.

"Oh I'm sure if he owns up it could be dealt with by your department." Joan was quick to say but added again that he shouldn't be doing that job.

She was assured that somebody would be coming to see her at the shop and to make sure she was there.

"We close at four today." She stated.

"Don't worry, it will be before then."

"That'll fix him." She thought. "He'll have a job finding work in that field by the time I've finished with him."

As far as she was concerned they could send who they liked and if they insisted on questioning Beaty, she wouldn't remember anything, and Maria couldn't confirm it because she didn't think she was concentrating on much that day apart from what her old man was up to.

Next she rang Maria's firm and asked for personnel. There she said almost in tears that her niece had stayed at her place and now money was missing and could they ask her about it. She knew that they would refuse and say it wasn't their place to enquire but it was enough to sow the seeds of doubt as to her honesty. And that's all it often took.

She'd saved the best till last. Phil answered the phone to hear a hysterical woman on the end of the line accusing Dick of raping her and saying that the police would be arresting him.

With the way the evil was twisting her mind, she wasn't even reasoning what she was doing. She thought doubt would be enough to ruin those who were making her life a misery which is exactly how this horrible cell worked. The subject really did believe everything they were feeding into the mind however wrong it was. The real nature of Joan would never have heard a word against any of her family and stood up for them, but suddenly they were all plotting against her and she must stand up for herself. Melba was saddened by this and was fighting all the way to get her released from this nightmare but every time she seemed to make progress, the evil seemed to rise up and squash everything. And this was one case, but it was being activated all over the area so decent people were being used to spread distrust, hatred and even abuse until life would be unbearable.

Midday seemed to take ages to arrive and Amy was out of the building as soon as possible. She had to find out what was going on with Cyn. As she reached the end of her road there was a cordon across the street.

"I've got to get through. I live here." She pleaded with the policeman who was guarding it.

"Sorry miss. No one allowed in."

At that point he was joined by a plain clothes man who was obviously also a cop. He had a list in his hand, spoke to the uniformed man, looked towards her then came over. Everyone else was clamouring to see what was going on.

"What's your name?"

Amy told him.

"Address?"

Again she answered.

"Let her through."

"Oh thank you." She started to say.

"This way."

"But I live over....."

"This way." He repeated and ushered her toward a police vehicle. "In there please."

It was like a mini office with two officers busily going over something.

"What's happened? Is Cyn alright? Please tell me."

She was ignored for a moment then he said "These officers would like to talk to you."

With that he left the van and she was facing two women officers.

"So, you're a friend of ....Cynthia Wade?" She checked the name on one of the papers.

"Yes. I know her but we aren't best friends at the moment. Why?"

"When did you last see her?"

Amy thought for a minute.

"Not for a day or so I think."

"So you didn't see her yesterday?"

"No."

"Did you see a car that you didn't recognise round here yesterday or anyone you didn't know?"

She shook her head wishing they would tell her what was going on.

"That will be all for now. You can go to your house. One of us will come with you but stick around. We may need to talk to you again."

"But..but is she ok?"

"That's all for now."

She was escorted to her home watched from the cordon by onlookers. Some called out, some even shouted abuse but she was told to ignore them.

When they got to her door the officer asked if she could come for a minute.

"It's easier talking when you feel comfy isn't it?" She sounded quite friendly. "I've brought you here because you can relax."

"Oh?" Amy wasn't understanding this very well.

They sat down.

"Amy, your friend, Cynthia was found dead last night. I'm sorry."

"What? Oh no. Where?"

"I can't go into the details but the press have the fact that it was in a back alley in the centre of town."

Amy was visibly shocked. "Not at home then?"

"No. But I expect you're wondering why we are here."

"I suppose so."

"In a case like this," she didn't say murder on purpose "we have to look into everything."

"I can't believe it." Amy was staring into space.

The officer didn't need it spelling out what Amy's connection was and offered a word of warning.

"That's the problem you see, when women on the game get into the wrong company. Often ends this way."

If she hoped Amy would take this as a lesson she was on a loser, for all Amy could see was that Cyn was dead. Not that she could be in line for the same fate if she wasn't careful.

"Will you be alright? Is there anyone you would like to sit with you?"

The officer hoped this may bring someone else out of the shadows.

"No. I'll ring my friend and talk to her."

"Who's that then?"

"Maria, she's really nice."

"Where does she live?"

Before long the officer had Maria's full name and her home address.

"You get some rest now."

As she left the officer had a number that would eventually lead to Dick who after all was one of Cyn's clients.

It didn't take long for local radio to announce that a local prostitute had been found dead possibly murdered and the area was buzzing. The police had called at Dick and Maria's home but both were at work. However they did have Maria's mobile number. She was very wary but agreed to meet the officer at tea break as long as someone came with her. She was very concerned it could be a bogus call, so her office manager suggested she ring the police station to verify the officer. As this seemed to check out, the manager offered to go with her, not to pry but to show some support so Maria wasn't on her own. Obviously she still hoped she would find out but didn't want to appear too eager.

"I didn't want to tell them where I was living in case they were crooks." She said.

The manager nodded. "Very wise, especially as you're at your mum's now."

They were told to go to the car park and a plain clothes officer would identify herself. They would then sit in an unmarked car. Both women were there on time and were soon approached by a detective who said she would prefer to speak to Maria alone but if she wasn't happy with it, her friend could stay.

"I think I'll be alright now, thank you." She turned to her manager who was a bit disappointed but was determined to way lay her on the way back to find out as much as she could.

As soon as they had settled, the officer explained that this could be a bit delicate but she did have to get the facts. After explaining what had happened she told her that her friend Amy had given her details to them.

"Well, she's not a close friend, and why would she give you my phone number?"

"She was in considerable shock and we asked if there was anyone she would like to sit with her. She said there wasn't but would like to phone you."

"Oh I see. So…..um…why would you need to speak to me then?"

"Well, and this is the delicate bit. The woman was a prostitute and we have learned that your friend was sometimes working with her."

"Well I can't say I'm that surprised. But I still don't see…" Maria was getting a bit confused. It was racing through her mind as to what else Amy, her so called friend had said.

The officer looked at her closely before she spoke again.

"From other information we've received, it appears that your husband was also a frequent visitor to the deceased."

Now it made sense.

"You're not saying he…."

"I'm not saying anything at this point. But it does rather put him into the mix so to speak. Just for the record can you tell me where you were last night?"

"Me? Am I under suspicion now? I never met the woman, couldn't even describe her."

"It's not that. But we have to check everything out including other people's alibis."

" Oh. Because I was at home on my own until my husband came home then I went to my mum's. That's where I'm staying now because she isn't well."

There was a pause before the next question.

"Is that the only reason?"

"What?"

"Did you have another reason to leave home?"

"Such as?" Maria was feeling awkward and under pressure.

"Well, for instance, did your husband say he was going out again?"

"No."

"You say he had come home. Where had he been?"

This was difficult. She really didn't know but that would sound as if she was hiding something.

"Well?" The officer prompted.

"He'd been away for the weekend."

"Oh where?"

"Look all I can tell you is what he told me."

"Which was?"

Maria could now reply honestly.

"He said he was driving his boss and his wife to see her, oh a relative I think and it meant he had to stay as well."

The other woman's look said it all.

"And you believed that?"

"Not really, but what could I do?"

There was quite a long pause while the detective made a few notes.

"I appreciate this isn't easy and you can see why I preferred you to be on your own, for your sake because I have to ask this. Did you have any suspicion that that he could have been with the deceased woman for the weekend?"

"No, not really."

"And you don't know, after you left if he was going back out. He didn't say anything to suggest it I mean."

"No. I never gave it a thought. Is it important?"

"Well, it seems at the moment that there is no one to verify his whereabouts after you left," she paused for a moment before adding "and the woman's body was found in the early hours of Monday."

"Oh my God. You're not saying, no he couldn't. He may not be the best husband but he wouldn't do anything like that."

They exchanged a few more words as the officer explained that they would obviously have to visit him and told her not to speak to him about it in the meantime. This was academic as there was already another officer at the garage interviewing him who would be aware if a call or message was sent to him during that time as his phone was on full view, they had made sure of that.

When the male detective was going through Dick's recent activities man to man, it came to the weekend he was away.

"So just where was it you went?"

"I don't know. A big house near Westborough, but you can't see it from the road."

"And who took you?"

"Some friends."

As soon as it got to the names, Dick knew he had a problem. He could only say what they had called themselves but didn't want to go into the sordid details of which sex they were.

"So in fact it was a dirty weekend."

"Well……"

"Oh come on, we've all done at some time haven't we?"

"Well….."

Even with prodding, Dick couldn't give any more information as to their identities and he certainly wasn't going to divulge what had gone on. He wanted to forget all about it.

The cop then went on to when Dick had got home and asked the same as his female counterpart regarding whether or not Dick had left the house once his wife had gone to her mother's.

"No I had a shower and went to bed. I was tired."

"I bet you were." There was still the innuendo in the tone hoping to bring him out a bit more but he was tight lipped.

"Did you ring anyone? Text anyone?"

"Nobody. I'd got to get up for work and I needed some sleep."

"Didn't get much then, while you were away I mean."

"No. Look why are you asking me all these questions. What's going on?"

Here was the breather before the blow.

"So, you say you were on your own all night at home, you didn't go out." This was a statement not a question. There was a significant pause before the next bit.

"You must have heard on the local radio the body of a woman was found in an alley in the centre of town."

"We have music on all day."

"She was found in the early hours of this morning."

"That's bad. Why are you telling me this? Hey hang on, is that why you were asking if I'd left home? What's it got to do with me?"

His mind was racing, it couldn't be Zena because she wasn't a woman, so why was he being questioned?

"The full details haven't been released yet, but from information we've received we understand you knew the lady, shall we say intimately."

"Now wait a minute you can't come in here accusing me. Are you saying I could have killed her? I don't even know who you're talking about."

"But the fact remains you don't have an alibi do you?"

"So I'm a suspect?"

"Everyone is at this point. Oh I don't suppose it will hurt to tell you, it will be released shortly anyway, the lady was a Cynthia Hobbs."

The detective watched as the colour drained from Dick's face.

"That confirms what I thought." He didn't actually say it but it was written all over his face.

He took down all Dick's contact details and left him with a strict warning not to go off an any more dirty weekends for now and to be available at all time.

"You'll be hearing from us again." Was the parting shot leaving Dick lost for words. After all that had happened, now this.

"Someone up there doesn't like me." He thought as he went to clear up.

The evil now attached to Dick was enjoying every minute of this and couldn't wait for the next instalment. It wasn't so much the fact of what horrors he could inflict on others, but what he would endure himself. Whereas those now controlling Joan wanted to be the perpetrators, this sadistic lot wallowed in watching him squirm. They were almost begging the cops to lock him up.

The angels were very familiar with these tactics along with many others so it was always imperative to know just what kinds were operating around you. Melba, Joan's guardian was worried over the speed at which Joan was being controlled and also the power of it.

Why would any force need her? But of course people weren't singled out. If the evil was planning a mass attack on an area, they would make a bulk collection so anyone could be roped in. The easiest targets were always those with an axe to grind, or ones who were out for retaliation or revenge and there were plenty of those.

Often the objective could go back years. If a wrong had been done, the hatred would fester long after the person had gone to the spirit world, then reinstate itself aiming at a relative or contact from years before so nobody would know why they had been selected. So if Joan or others had been picked for such a task they may have no connection themselves to the fiend who was using them, they were merely a tool that would be thrown away when the job was complete. All she would be aware of was what she imaged to be her own feelings. That was always the sad part. The innocent became the guilty.

Chapter 12

Maria went home to Beaty's feeling furious but she had to hide her feelings in front of her mum. At one time she would have understood but now it wouldn't sink in.

Not only had that bum hole of a husband lied about his weekend away, but now it had been brought home to her door with the unfortunate demise of one of his floosies. Added to that, her so called friend Amy had directed the police straight to her. And how many lies had she told? All of a sudden she seemed to have been dragged into a murder case because of these two.

"What's up?" Beaty's voice broke into her thoughts as she got the tea.

"Oh nothing mum, just busy at work, that's all."

"Alright, if you say so. Well, don't overdo it."

"I won't mum." She kissed the top of her head as she passed.

"It's lovely having you here." She whispered but Maria had to leave the room as she felt the tears coming.

When they had eaten and the washing up was done Maria sat opposite Beaty and said "Mum, it's nothing to worry about but, well I don't know what Dick's been up to, but someone he knows…" She didn't know how to put it.

"There's been a murder." Beaty piped up.

"What?"

"Saw it on the news just before you came. It was in town, street girl."

Maria wanted to ask how she'd remembered that but that didn't seem too important considering how her memory came and went.

"Yes mum, well it seems that Dick may have known her."

"Oh. That's how it is, is it?"

"How what is, oh never mind. The thing is mum the police have already asked me some questions and I just wanted to warn you in case they came here."

"Well I don't know anything. I've not been out."

"No not you mum, me. They have been talking to me."

"Why, you didn't do it."

"Because I'm Dick's wife they automatically think I know everything he gets up to."

"Well you don't want to do that."

"No I know." Maria had to smile at her mum's response. "But I don't think he has an alibi you see."

"Well it's time he got one then."

The moment of understanding had gone, but Beaty had lifted Maria somewhat with her innocence.

Her mind drifted back to work for a moment. The head of personnel had informed her of her aunt's phone call saying they had told her they couldn't do anything about it. Fortunately they had known each other for years so Maria's honesty was never in doubt. The lady said that with the way the mum was going she wondered if the same thing was happening to her aunt. Not knowing quite what was happening with Joan at the moment, Maria seized on the idea and said she thought that could be quite possible. After all she hadn't been her usual self and there had been a severe change of character. They had never fallen out to such an extent before. So that was at least one of Joan's plans that hit the floor. The good had influenced it.

Amy was hoping that none of this would interfere with her new job on Wednesday. She had made up her mind that she would ring in to work and say her mum was poorly and she had to look after her. Also she was praying that the police presence would have gone as she didn't want to be followed to where she was going to be picked up. It didn't occur to her that ones fetching her wouldn't go anywhere near the place if it wasn't safe.

Word was spreading throughout the spirit world that the little evil cells were being placed at strategic positions and not randomly as it first appeared. The high levels had seen this before but had to wait until they were certain as to what was happening otherwise if they went in half cocked they could destroy a whole operation. The likes of Joan alone meant nothing, but when everyone was in position and there were thousands just waiting for the word of command, it could result in major terrorism and even natural disasters. But nobody could see it coming because the threats didn't seem to warrant huge interest. It would soon be time for the good forces to move in and take action but had to be kept on low key or the evil would pick up the vibes so all plans had to be cloaked.

Dick had phoned Maria a couple of times and although she discussed the death of Cyn, refused to consider going back. The conversation was usually the same.

"You didn't want me then and the only reason you want me now is to do your washing and cook your meals."

She wasn't holding back and she didn't care if her mum heard as she'd forget it the next minute.

"And if you think you're sticking that thing in me after where it's been, think again. And I'm getting myself checked over in case you've passed something on to me."

He had no answer really but threw it back at her that it was all her fault, because if she'd satisfied him he wouldn't have had to go elsewhere.

In the end she decided there was no point in talking unless it was to discuss a divorce and when she would fetch the rest of her things. She also told him in no uncertain terms that she didn't want to be drawn into his sordid little life and didn't want the police coming round every time he messed up. She couldn't resist asking one question at the end of the last conversation.

"Tell me, have you shagged Amy as well?"

"Who?"

"Oh don't come the innocent. That woman's partner in crime. The one that was supposed to be my friend."

"Can't place her off hand."

"Well it doesn't matter. You're both the scum of the earth. Now your regular has gone, perhaps you should look her up."

He still couldn't see what he had done. All the fake promises that Maria had thought he meant were just a load of empty words. She didn't believe anything he said now, and when trust has gone, there's nothing left. He had killed every ounce of love in her and there was no way it could ever be repaired.

Tuesday brought some changes in many ways. The police had a suspect who had confessed to the murder. He said it was an accident and he hadn't meant to kill the woman but he was drunk and it had happened before he realised. The evidence itself held up everything he said and so he was charged.

To say Dick breathed a huge sigh of relief was an understatement. Although he knew he was innocent, it meant the police would stop delving into his weekend drama.

Maria received a call from the officer that had spoken to her but when she put the phone down she had the feeling that it wasn't just a pleasantry, more that the woman was trying to find out more about her husband. This made her wonder what else he'd been up to. It was like living on a knife edge. You didn't know what was going to turn up next.

For some reason the police seemed interested in where Dick had gone that weekend and didn't believe he was telling the whole story. They wanted names, proper ones not made up to keep their anonymity. Even if he had known he had no intention of telling them but out of curiosity he had an idea. When Zena had left her car for a job to be done at the garage she must have also left details. He chose the right moment when Phil had gone to the bank and looked through the records. On the day it was booked in the name was a Mrs. Black and a mobile phone number. Where was the address? There had to be one for the bill. Phil's name was against the job although he hadn't done it. So he went onto the computer to check the invoice, but there wasn't one. His mind started turning. He can't have charged her for some reason. But he could hardly ask him. Quickly he put everything back as it was and went to start the next job.

Frank walked into the charity shop to be greeted by Evie.
"On your own?" He asked.
"No, Joan's out the back. Do you want her?"
"Not particularly. How's trade."

"Oh, bit quiet at the moment, hardly needs two of us."

He wandered round looking at various things then Joan appeared.

"Oh. I didn't know you were here." She looked a bit embarrassed.

"Didn't expect to see me did you?"

"Well it's always nice when you come in."

"Is it? Did you expect me to bring some jewellery in for you to sell?"

Joan stood there frozen to the spot. She had promised herself she would show him up but suddenly the position was reversed.

"You're very quiet." He had her fixed in his gaze. "Bit different when you rang with false accusations. Well I'm here. What have you got to say now?"

"I'm not sure what….."

"Oh please," he interrupted "don't make yourself look any more ridiculous that you already are. You do realise you can be done for slander."

"It…it was a mistake, we found it after you'd gone."

"Oh really." His tone could have cut the air. "And were you as hasty to ring again and tell them?"

"Well I haven't had time, I've been here."

He gave the most ugly smile she had ever seen.

"Well, you could have used that phone over there. The one you used to accuse me. Remember?"

She stood there her mouth open.

The evil forces were putting words into her head but the good ones were erasing them as quickly.

As he went out of the door he turned to Evie and said "I'll see you again." Then to Joan "Pity I can't say the same to you."

With that he'd gone.

"What the fu… I mean what did he mean?" Evie hastily changed the wording she almost used.

"I've really no idea." Joan had a very good idea. She was about to get the push.

The thing that stuck in her mind was how he had changed from the limp lettuce that he had been at Beaty's to this upstart who thought he ruled the world.

It certainly gave the two something to talk about for the rest of the afternoon.

It is a known practice used by the higher levels of the spirit world to take action when an evil virus is threatening an area. Unfortunately some of the bad forces are as powerful and can not only block such an attack but to turn it around and wipe out the good in return. Therefore it is only used if disaster threatens and has to be expedited solely from above. The angels on lower levels have to cloak any thought of it once a request has been logged.

Some liken it to social media. If a general post is made, it is there for all to view, but if you select friends, only they should see it. Also on an offshoot from this you can have a supposedly private conversation with one person alone. It can work the same in spirit. Experienced ones can channel to a specific point but there will always be the hackers. Therefore extreme caution has to be employed at all times.

Sofia and a few of her position had agreed that she would put in a request for a surge. This would entail an entire sweep of the area, taking out the evil and dispatching them. It didn't include the day to day wayward spirits who delighted in upsetting the smooth running of people's lives, but the type that were now threatening this part.

As soon as she had placed the requirement, she wiped it from her memory. She would have no more communication on the subject so it would be a waiting game and would come as a surprise to her at first, but then her spiritual memory would be restored from higher sources.

If all seemed fairly quiet to the earth dwellers it was nothing to the planning and arranging that was going on around them for the spirit world is a very busy place and has to be kept in order.

Dick now felt he was treading water, not knowing where his life was going from here. He missed Maria but still hankered after the excitement of playing around and he couldn't understand why she made such a fuss about it. All of a sudden he felt free, he could do as he liked without a third degree all the time. But when he turned round for a clean shirt he had to take what was there, not the one he wanted. That was still in the clothes basket. And he had to get his own food.

"Well, she walked out." He said out loud. "She'll want me before I want her. Then she'll come crawling back."

He still couldn't see that she had left because of him and he could only look at it as her being selfish. But the Dick's of this world are never in the wrong. It's always about them, and how badly they have been treated. They criticise people they thought were friends but have now ditched them but can't see how they in turn have treated them to cause this reaction. And they would never change.

Beaty was enjoying her daughter being around, when she could remember but at least she was being looked after. Maria was finding it much more peaceful but she was in turmoil. She had loved Dick so much but he had killed all the feeling by his lack of consideration, and now it had turned to utter disgust. There was no going back. To her he was dirty.

She was well aware already that it would be soul destroying when her mum couldn't remember anything but she would ask for help when it was too much for her. At one time Joan would have been sharing the load but she wasn't the same person, so was this her true self coming out? The only thing was to take each day as it came and cope with it that way.

As one day rolled into another, Wednesday was upon them. Amy went to work in the morning then rang in to her evening job to say she wasn't feeling well. She'd thought of various excuses for her absence but ended up with this one. She was being picked up at seven and was counting the hours with mixed feelings, but the lure of big money kept coming to the fore.

It was still fairly warm as the summer was coming to an end so she decided she needn't bother with a coat and there was no sign of rain so she would just wear her new outfit, second hand but new to her. She knew she should have something to eat but somehow she had to force it down as the nerves kicked in.

As it was still light when she left home, she hoped too many wouldn't see her because after recent happenings they would soon work out what she was doing, as if they didn't know already. She hurried out of her road then had a bit of a walk to the pick up area which was just off the main road. Almost on the dot a large van pulled up, the front passenger got out and opened the back door.

"In." Was all he said.

There were long seats down each side and she sat on the end near the door which was the only vacant one.

"Belt up." The voice came from further in.

Now the doors were shut there was very little light coming in from the window to the cab but as her eyes became accustomed she made out four women on the opposite bench and three on her side. The one opposite her didn't look to bad but the others seemed really hard old cows. Amy fastened her seat belt and there was silence. It was as though nobody was allowed to speak so she certainly wasn't going to say anything.

They'd been going for some time and Amy was wondering just how far this place was when they suddenly turned off the road and she was glad now of the seat belt as she would have been thrown across the van without doubt. Dick was would have recognised the property immediately.

They went down the drive and round to the back of the manor house. All was quiet for a moment then the doors were opened. Amy forgot to undo her seat belt and the delay caused some tut tuts from the others.

"Right," the man from the front passenger seat ordered, "up the back stairs, follow those, they know." He indicated to the four old bags so Amy and the other girl followed in silence. As soon as they were out the van disappeared out of sight.

They had to move to keep up with the others who seemed as though they must get there as soon as possible.

"How much further?" Amy whispered.

"Hope not much." The other one answered.

Eventually they reached the top floor where they were met by a woman who Dick would have recognised as Luce.

"You four – as usual." She nodded for them to go to the far end of the corridor.

"You two. Listen up. That end," she pointed to the disappearing four, "is a bathroom, don't go in it, it's also a wet room. They work in pairs, always in those two rooms. Now to save going over it twice, both of you come in here." The door was marked A. The room seemed very sparse but clean.

"Right. Sink, paper towels, condoms. Waste bin, put everything in here and I mean everything, plumbing isn't brilliant up here." She turned to a large cupboard and pulled the door open.

"At the bottom, put your own stuff in that box. Here, clean sheet, change it before your next one, only if it's marked though. Put any dirty ones on that shelf."

She slammed the door and was making her way to the door as she spoke.

"Remember you are just straight lays. That's all they pay for, that's all they get. No kinky business that's extra, but not from you. Or we'll have a riot on our hands. You, Amity are in here, you Belle are next door. You have 40 minutes with each, then use five minutes to clean up then the next will be up. You only have three each tonight. Oh yes the toilet is the one you passed at the top of the stairs, it's for you and the customers so keep it clean."

The two looked at each other but before they had time to think Luce called "Your first one's in five minutes. Be ready, and no nosing anywhere else. The expensive ones are downstairs, they don't want you gawping. It's all privacy here. Understood?" And she had gone.

Belle said "Well I need a wee."

"Me too, after you."

When she went back into the room, Amy noticed the screen on the wall. Funny it hadn't been mentioned but perhaps it was nothing to do with them. Also there was a clock and now she knew the importance of this.

There was a timid tap on the door. When she opened it she thought it was someone to do with the place but he said "Amity?"

"Yes." Then it dawned on her. "Oh come in."

For the first time she felt so alone. She was in charge, there was no Cyn to tell her what to do.

"I hope I don't mess up." She thought but smiled a very forced smile and ushered her first customer into her room.

"Are you a new one?" He was eyeing her up and down almost drooling. "Must say I like you better than the last one. She was ugly."

He was already undressing so that saved her the bother of whether to help or not and then she saw it. The screen had come to life and the woman was really giving the man the works. It wasn't intentional but it served as a lesson for Amy who was staring at it taking note of some things she'd never thought of.

"Oh good, they've got a new one. I was getting sick of the other pair." The man was also drooling and rising to the action already. It didn't take him long to shoot and Amy was wondering what to do for the other thirty five minutes but she was being paid, and even if he wasn't very attractive this was work and would pay good money. She'd been promised.

Having remembered her instructions she made sure the used johnny was put in the big pedal bin and suddenly noticed he was at the side of her peeing in the sink.

"It's alright, I always do this." He smiled. "Probably wouldn't make it to the lav."

When he'd finished he said "Do you want to wash it before we go again?"

Her mind was racing. By a straight lay did they mean only once? She'd never had to follow rules before, she just did it but this was different and she hadn't got anyone to ask. She couldn't very well race down the corridor, tap on the door and ask how many times, could she? Then a thought hit her. "If he's paying for forty minutes, I suppose it doesn't matter how many, but how does he manage it?" Any man she'd serviced only did it once so she had thought that was the norm.

"Well, are you?" His question made her jump.

"Oh you can. Do you want to watch the film for a bit?"

"Do I? I say this is a good one this is. Wish I'd got his sausage."

Sure enough it didn't take him long to rise up again and they were off.

"Wonder if they charge for the jackets?" She thought.

Where he got his energy or his fluid supply was beyond her for the next time was even more energetic and he certainly packed a punch. When it was coming to the time for him to be dressed and off, she was almost relieved. She opened the door and expected him just to go and that was it. He stopped, shook her hand and told her it had been extremely enjoyful and he hoped to see her again.

Really he had been a very nice man and probably in business but a different kind to this. Remembering her instructions she checked the bed, it seemed alright so she got ready for the next. There was quite a pause so she wandered out to see if anyone was coming up the back stairs.

The top floor had been the servant's quarters and below it was floor was where Dick had been entertained. His room and the one which Josh and Luce had used were the luxury suites and demanded top rate from the customers, and the three in between were less expensive but still costly and all sorts of requirements were provided for. The same video was played in all rooms and being the latest was getting its first airing. Whether it was watched or not didn't matter but some relied on it for initial stimulation.

Belle was also waiting for her next one.
"Bit late." She whispered to Amy.
"Mine too, perhaps they're coming together."
"Quick here they come."
They hustled back to their own rooms and as Amy was about to close her door she caught sight of Belle's next customer. Her mouth dropped open for she recognised him as the one Cyn had told her was Dick's boss. So Phil was in the next room. Her client arrived straight after, another older man but so what? She didn't have to like them.

They had finished the job and he was sitting on the bed watching the screen.
"Unusual tat." He got up to have a closer look. "Nice, wonder where he got it."
This made Amy curious. Hadn't Cyn remarked on one of her men having one that she hadn't seen before? No names of course. She stood up now and went over to get a closer look.
"Damn, they've changed the shot. She's tasty though." He was watching Zena now. "Wouldn't have minded a bit of that."
"Thanks very much." Amy had said it before she realised.

"Oh no, you were good. Just window shopping love."

His time was up and she couldn't help thinking what a friendly person he was and why did he have to come to a place like this. Surely he could find himself a decent woman of his own.

In the next room Phil was enjoying normal sex but wishing he could run to the more interesting stuff downstairs but at the prices quoted it was way out of his league. But at least here it was properly organised and there was no way anyone would know he'd been.

He was underneath Belle which gave him a view of the screen when suddenly the garden scene was being played. Although Belle was doing a good job his attention was glued to what he was watching. It was a distance shot, but there was no doubt as to the identity of the man who was apparently parting company with his most prized possession.

He managed to let her finish the job satisfactorily but his eyes kept returning to the antics being played out. Suddenly it all became clear. Now he knew what Dick must have been doing at the weekend and with Zena! When she had got him the contact to come to this place he thought it was because they had something special going on which was why he hadn't charged her for the car repairs. He didn't know at that time that she wasn't all she made out to be. Now all the taunts of the lads at work were ringing in his head because he had just been watching this so called woman performing with…..Dick! He must be the man in the video although his face was out of shot. Did he know about her, or him rather? He must have found out at some point.

Now all Phil wanted to do was get as far away from here as possible and never come back. How he was going to look Dick in the eye he didn't know, but he'd worry about that later. Now he must get home.

As Amy's customer left she wondered if Belle had finished with Dick's boss so she hovered with the door partly open. Almost immediately he came out and now she was sure. Definitely him which surprised her a bit. If she was at the cheap end, surely he would have gone a bit up market in his tastes but maybe it was out of his price range. After all she didn't know how much they paid on the floor below.

Before the next ones arrived, Luce appeared on the landing.

"Right, when you've finished with the last ones, make sure the room is tidy then get your butts downstairs. Go in the kitchen, make yourselves a drink and you'll get paid before you go. You'll have to wait for the other four, they have more to do, then you'll be taken back. You speak of this to no one. Deny everything. We don't exist. Understood?"

They both nodded in agreement.

"I'll send them up then." And Luce disappeared down the stairs.

Amy's last one was as nervous as she had been. Obviously his first time so it gave her a bit of confidence. She reckoned he must be younger than her and after a few minutes she realised something.

"You ever done it before?" She said very kindly.

"Oh yes loads of times."

"Really. What's your favourite?"

"My favourite?" He was lost.

"Position of course."

"Oh, yes, um well the usual one is best don't you think."

"Oh bloody hell a learner." She thought.

Her attention had been on him throughout the session and after she had managed to break him in and they were catching their breath, her eyes moved to the screen again. There was something about the man that was getting to her. She felt she knew him but couldn't quite put her finger on it.

She and Belle went down the stairs together and got a drink.

"Oh biccies as well." Amy said.

"Are they for us?"

"Must be."

Luce came in and handed them an envelope each.

"Do we check it?" Belle asked.

"Up to you."

The two felt it seemed a bit rude to so put them in their bags.

"You've been paid for how many you've had. If you move up to the specials you get paid for the night. That's where you really earn."

With that she left.

"I'm going to look." Amy ripped open the envelope and pulled out seventy five pounds."

"I've got the same." Belle said.

"But I was told it would be big money." Amy was hoping for more.

"I expect that's when you work on that other floor, and I bet you those other four get more."

"Well at least we've had it now, not had to wait." Amy was thinking back to the other episode.

After a while the others came down and soon they were all bundled back into the van and taken home.

When Amy got back she didn't feel as elated as she thought she would. She knew she was at the bottom of the ladder, but would she ever make it to the top?

Chapter 13

During the night the surge had been executed and when people woke on Thursday morning, moods were very different. Joan was very aware that she had been unbearable and it upset her. What had made her so nasty? For a start she must speak to Maria, not really knowing how she was going to start but it had to be done. She picked the phone up several times and put it down again before she actually rang.

"Hello, Maria? Look, this isn't easy I don't know what's happened to me over the past few days but I wasn't me."

"No, that was pretty obvious."

"I know I've upset you but can I come round at lunchtime when you're there. I do want to help you know, and you've got a lot on with Beaty."

"If you want." Was the only reply.

She wasn't going to explain that she had moved in or why.

Joan was hoping she was going to say that it was all ok and not to worry but that didn't come. Maria still had her husband very much on her mind and as long as her mum was looked after, she still had to give her marriage a lot of consideration. This was a big upheaval for she knew she could never go back to him.

"Well I'll see you then." Joan put the phone down. "Oh dear this isn't going to be easy." She thought.

She got ready to go to the charity shop wondering if she still had a job. This was still on her mind when Evie breezed in, and after a quick "Morning" she told her that she felt she may not be required soon.

"Oh I wouldn't give that a thought." Evie put her jacket on the rack in the staff area.

"Well I'm not so sure." Joan was recalling Frank's last words.

"Oh haven't you heard. My friend told me he's going."

"He's going?" Joan emphasised the 'he'.

"Oh yes, It seems he only works in one place for a short time then moves on. Not sure where he's off to though."

"Oh so that's probably what he meant." She felt a bit easier now then turning back to Evie asked "Are you here all lunch time?"

"Yeah. Why?"

"Could you manage on your own, only there's something I have to do."

"Course. No probs."

The air in the shop had lightened considerably since the day before.

When she pulled up outside Beaty's she was relieved to see Maria's car but guilt still ran high. She let herself in and called out to let them know she was there. Beaty was sitting in her usual chair having her lunch and Joan couldn't help noticing how fresh and clean she looked. After the usual greeting she plucked up the courage to go into the kitchen.

"Only me." She said softly.

Without offering a 'hello' Maria said without turning "Just made a tea if you'd like one."

"Maria, what can I say? I know I've not been myself and I'm going to the doc to see if he can put an answer to it."

"Let's hope whatever it was has passed." Maria didn't turn as she was trying to hold it together and any kindness would have made her crumble and she didn't want to appear weak or break down.

Joan's arms went to her shoulders and she hugged her from the back and now she was the one who broke.

Within seconds they were both in each other's arms sobbing as though their hearts would break.

"I shouldn't have left you to cope. You're at work and to have to keep coming backwards and forwards like this."

"Aunt Joan. I live here now."

"Oh. Well, you didn't have to do that, with your work and Dick."

"I've left him and I'm not going back so you see Mum is getting all the care she can while I'm not at work."

"Oh I'm so sorry. I didn't realise. I..I. "

"Can't go into it all now, there's going to be a lot to sort out and I've got to be strong enough to do it."

Joan looked at her. "Well one thing you can rely on me being here to give you a break sometimes. You can't do it all as she gets worse."

"What are you two squabbling about?" The call made them both smile.

"Just talking mum, coming now." Maria had to smile and wiped her face on the hand towel then whispered "Be careful in front of her, she picks things up."

Joan also had to compose herself but in her mind she still couldn't understand what had come over her. But one thing was for sure, it would never happen again.

This is where evil doesn't do itself any favours for when people have come under its shadow and escaped, they build a barrier to stop it infiltrating again, but of course they don't realise the underlying cause.

Melba was relieved. It didn't matter how it had come about. She had her result.

The police were still curious as to where Dick had been as they liked to keep their eye on everything in their area. Sometimes the most unlikely venues had turned out to be drug contacts or weapon stashes so it had often paid not to discard any seemingly innocent information. All they had at the moment was 'a big house near Westborough but couldn't be seen from the road'.

They had asked local patrols to keep an eye open but it had drawn a blank. Those that knew the area reported that, with it all being private land many of the buildings wouldn't be visible. One they had visited that was owned by a celebrity was set back about half a mile from the road and behind trees so would never be spotted.

As they couldn't ask every land owner if they could view their property the next option was to use the helicopter crew who could photograph those with dwellings. But it was a huge area so it had to be narrowed down also they couldn't waste money on something that wasn't definite. One thing they did know from Dick was that it took about an hour to get there. They had a starting point so could plot a rough area if they could get the chopper. Failing that they may be able to enlist the help of the local flying club who often did aerial shots for various companies.

Of course there was the fact that what anyone did on their own premises was their own business provided it didn't annoy anyone else, and as this was out in the sticks, it was hardly likely to do that. It was simply the fact that those officers with a 'nose' for these things had a gut feeling there was much more to this than nipping off to a friend's house for a dirty weekend.

As soon as the last clients had gone from the manor it was time to await the arrival of 'The Man'. This was the boss who employed people to find clients and workers such as Amy. The venue was constantly moved so that he couldn't be traced. Zena, Luce and Josh were waiting in the lounge and were joined by the one who had acted as the cook, also the maids and the gardener.

"I'll be sorry to leave here." Zena said.

"You always say that." Josh laughed. "And then you'll like the next one even better."

Luce had got the money ready for collection and there was nothing more to do except watch for the car.

This was a lucrative business run by one who knew how to stay ahead of anyone who tried to trap him or track him down and he operated in a different way to anyone else. A skill he had mastered to perfection. Nobody would see the car arrive as he had his own route.

Some of these country mansions were connected with underground tunnels so a lot of illicit business went on without anyone being any the wiser. Years ago wenches had been transported for the master's delight and returned without anyone knowing thus maintaining the outward show of decency. What was delivered or despatched was anyone's guess and if people disappeared, one could only speculate as to how they had been hidden.

It was by this route that 'The Man' was due to arrive. The entrance/exit was in an old barn so it would seem that the vehicle had been parked in there. After collecting his loot he would return the same way and where he surfaced at the other end only he knew.

They stood quietly now until a faint noise was heard from near the fireplace. That was the signal. Taking the money they all went out through the staff entrance and made their way to the barn. 'The

Man' didn't get out of the car and released the door to the boot which provided the only light. Luce went to the rear and placed the money in a certain box as always then she returned to the others. The boot was closed from a control inside the car. They now stood in darkness and 'The Man' partly opened the passenger window so he could be heard.

"Did you enjoy this one?"

They all acknowledged.

"Time to go. Until the next."

That was their sign to leave and he always waited until he knew they had actually departed. Without any sound they all moved to the back of the house and took a few steps onto the lawn. Within seconds they had gone, vanished with no trace of them ever having been there. Although he was in body he had complete control of these spirits and conducted various businesses using them. They could take any temporary form which is why they were never suspected although he had to keep their visits limited so as not to be traced.

These weren't the only group, he had several but not necessarily all working at the same time. With the money he made he could have lived a life of luxury but that would have attracted attention so he preferred to live a seemingly ordinary life hidden in plain sight. It was the control that gave him the buzz.

With them all despatched he turned his car into the bolt hole and made his way back along the tunnel to his exit. The car didn't look anything special from the outside which is why it never drew any attention.

"Time to move on to the next." Frank said to himself.

About the Author

Tabbie Browne grew up in the Cotswolds in central England which is where she gets the inspiration for her novels. Her father had very strong spiritual beliefs and she feels he guides her but always with a warning to stay in control of your own mind.

Her earliest recollection of writing was at primary school and it has seemed to play a part at significant times during her life. She thinks it is only when we are forced to take step back and unclutter our minds for a while we realise our potential. This point was proved when she slipped a disc, and being very immobile had to write in pencil as the ink would not flow upwards! At this time she wrote many comical poems which, when able again, performed to many audiences. Comedy is very difficult but you know if you are a success with a live audience.

In 1991 as a collector of novelty salt and pepper shakers, she realised there was no book in the UK devoted entirely to the subject. So she wrote one. Which meant she achieved the fact that it was the first of its kind in the country and it sold well to like collectors not only in the UK but in the USA.

Another large upheaval came when she was diagnosed with breast cancer, and due to the extreme energy draining, found it difficult to work for an employer. So she took a freelance journalist course and was pleased to have articles accepted, her main joy being the piece about her father and his life in the village. Again the inspiration area.

But the novels were eating away inside and drawing on her experience at stamp and coin fairs she wrote *'A Fair Collection'* which she serialised in the magazine 'Squirrels' for people who hoard things.

When she wrote 'White Noise Is Heavenly Blue' and its sequel 'The Spiral' she sat at the keyboard and the titles just came to her, as did the content of the books. There is no way she could write the plot first as she never knew what was coming next, almost as if somebody was dictating, and for that reason she could never change anything.

Loves:
Animals,
Also performing in live theatre and working as a tv supporting artiste.

Hates:
Bad manners,
Insincere people.

Printed in Great Britain
by Amazon